FAERY LOVES AND FAERY LAIS

AS TOLD BY

GARETH KNIGHT

SKYLIGHT PRESS

First published in Great Britain in 2012 by Skylight Press,
210 Brooklyn Road, Cheltenham, Glos GL51 8EA

Cover photography by Rebsie Fairholm
Designed and typeset by Rebsie Fairholm
Publisher: Daniel Staniforth

www.skylightpress.co.uk

Printed and bound in Great Britain by Lightning Source, Milton Keynes

British Library Cataloguing in Publication Data.
A catalogue record for this book is available from the British Library.

ISBN 978-1-908011-48-0

CONTENTS

Faery Tradition in Breton Lais

THE BRETON LAI is a relatively short narrative poem, usually accompanied by music, that appeared in France some time about the middle of the 12th century, spread by travelling musicians and story tellers called *jongleurs*. What we find important about them is that they contain a great deal of faery and supernatural lore deriving from Celtic myth, legend and folk tale.

There was also at this time a growing demand in courtly circles for long romances to be written and recited by court poets such as Chrétien de Troyes, who worked under the patronage of Countess Marie of Champagne and later Count Philip of Flanders, and who was one of the first to exploit the popularity of Arthurian legend, albeit to an aristocratic audience.

A major source for the romances of such professional courtiers were the lais told by the travelling jongleurs, who in turn derived their tales from the insular Celtic fringe of Ireland, Wales, Cornwall, and Brittany on the continental mainland. Whilst at the same time a courtly lady by the name of Marie de France, connected to the English court of Henry II, set about collecting a dozen Breton lais and rendering them into Old French.

Most of the lais we reproduce here in translation are however not the lais of Marie, but by unknown singer story tellers, which have thus escaped the courtly hand of Marie. Although she performed a great service in preserving such material, she felt constrained to refine it somewhat and even to secularise some of the supernatural elements. Her greater interest was in the psychological and moral dilemmas of the characters – and while this may make her an important figure in medieval literary studies it lessens her importance as a recorder of ancient popular belief and faery tradition.

In the anonymous lais we have a cruder and less sophisticated rendering of the stories but also more direct reportage of the marvels of the supernatural, which are taken for granted rather than subtly secularised.

The crux of these is to be found in the appearance and characteristics of the faery, or *fée*, a supernatural being, usually feminine, who is young, beautiful and richly dressed, and possesses magic powers to help a human being she likes and loves. There are also, however, male counterparts of the female faery, who may take the form of a young and handsome knight clad in red armour and riding a white charger (possibly with red ears) that is capable of galloping underwater or, on dry land, faster than a bird can fly.

The first mention of faeries in medieval French literature occurred in *Le Pelerinage de Charlemagne* (c.1140) where a "fée" is credited with making a magnificent bed coverlet, and in *L'Estoire des Engleis* (1136/7) by Geffrei Gaimar, who claimed that "Elfroed was so beautiful that Edelwold believed she must have been a faery".

We do not know the dates of the lais. The earliest one known, the Lai of the Horn, by a certain Robert Biket, is reckoned to date from 1150/75; and Marie de France is thought to have collected her lais some time between 1160 and 1199. Interestingly enough, Robert Biket's lai tells of a chastity test featuring a drinking horn which later appears in Arthurian legend as a ploy of Morgan le Fay.

The anonymous lais we feature in this book are of uncertain date. One, Tydorel, closely resembles Perceval in Chrétien de Troyes' famous romance *Le Conte del Graal* but features faery rather than human knights in the hero's famous early confrontation in the forest. Which version came first is a matter for conjecture.

Some lais show evidence of being crudely scripted narrative as might be the stock in trade of a modern stand-up comic, but whether this is evidence of being anterior to Marie de France's more finished literary renderings we cannot say. It has been suggested that some might have been deliberately roughened up to appear older than they actually are – but this seems unlikely. And of course they could appear rough and ready even if written well after the time of Marie de France. They catered to different audiences – Marie to the educated and aristocratic – the original lais presented to various audiences wherever a crowd could be gathered, in inn or market place or servants' hall.

Just as Arthurian legend, although featuring "the matter of Britain" was largely written in French, so in our own day faery tradition has been more seriously studied in French. Two important texts are *Les Fées au Moyen Age* by Laurence Harf-Lancner (Champion, Paris, 1984) and *La Fée á la Fontaine et á l'arbre* by Pierre Gallais (Rodopi, Amsterdam – Atlanta GA, 1992).

However, just as medieval sophisticates such as Chrétien de Troyes and Marie de France felt obliged to secularise the faery marvels – possibly for religious reasons – so modern commentators feel the same impulse for different reasons – Laurence Harf-Lancner regarding them as a 12th century literary invention and Pierre Gallais preferring the psychological route of archetypes of the unconscious. It has been left to traditionalists such as myself and R.J. Stewart and Wendy Berg to suggest taking them at face value – as in an earlier generation did W.B. Yeats, George Russell, Fiona Macleod and Ella Young. Whilst J.R.R.Tolkien's important essay *On Fairy-Stories* is also worth reading between the lines. As he says, "Faerie is a perilous land, and in it are pitfalls for the unwary and dungeons for the overbold." And adds "I have been hardly more than a wandering explorer (or trespasser) in the land, full of wonder but not of information." Although some of this wonder and indeed information is to be found in his fantasy fiction and also in our lais.

Faery lore has always been with us, indeed as long as faeries, but only in the last twenty years has it begun to return to prominence. This largely thanks to R.J. Stewart who has written some very practical books, from *The UnderWorld Initiation* in 1985, through *Earth Light* and *Power within the Land* in 1992, to *The Living World of Faery* in 1995 and *The Well of Light* in 2004.

These have been particularly stimulating because they show how it is possible to make the necessary connections by means of structured visualisations, particularly in conjunction with certain sites, such as standing stones, earthworks, forest paths, springs, pools, wells, woods, trees, meadows, crossroad tracks or the confluence of waters.

In the pursuit of otherworld experience we have, of course, to take care that any such contacts are not subjective fantasies. Faeries are not quite such wish fulfilment figures as they are sometimes made out to be, and so we should not regard the quest as some kind of otherworld dating agency. Those forlornly seeking fulfilment of unsatisfied desires should stick, for their own good, to the human sphere. If you cannot make it with one of your own kind then you are not likely to have much luck with one of the Shining Ones!

In my own experience the start of any worthwhile contact has come as something of a surprise. The initiative came from the other side. When I found myself whipped up into some kind of spiral of euphoric awareness, with aura lit up like a Christmas tree, to discover I was standing in muddy shoes over a spring, in close proximity to a rowan tree. Or coming across part of a hedgerow where trunks of oak and ash formed pillars each side of a hawthorn gateway, to find it open before me on the level of inner awareness.

First comes the experience, then the realisation. Following upon this, if you are lucky and play your cards right, a deepening relationship can form from which friendship, companionship, guidance and teaching may arrive. At any rate, to a born scribbler such as myself, the consequence has been the writing of *The Faery Gates of Avalon* and *Melusine of Lusignan and the Cult of the Faery Woman* (R.J. Stewart Books 2008 and 2010) followed up with a translation of André Lebey's modern version of *The Romance of the Faery Melusine* (Skylight Press 2011). All of which are meant to be subtle guides and stimuli to action rather than otherworldly street maps.

Above all they seek to be modern. The study of old traditions of faery lore that have come down to us in legend and ballad can be very fascinating and indeed instructive but they speak of other times and other conditions. The faery world moves on as does the human one, and means of intercommunication now are not the same as once they might have been.

Older forms of tradition speak not so much of intercommunication as of complete transition. Either a human is lured into faery land – or a faery enters the human world – visitors in an alien environment to that in which they were born. And such adventures tend to end in grief. Either the human being cannot find the way back, or if successful crumbles to dust, having been away for a very long time indeed in a different time dimension. Or the faery is driven back to fairyland because the human being breaks faith in some way, unable or unwilling to fulfil the conditions of such an unusual relationship.

This is the ground base of faery tradition that we find in the Breton lais. And although it speaks of older times and older ways there is much to be gained from a knowledge and appreciation of it. Just as the perennial popularity of Arthurian legend can be put down to the Otherwordly dynamics that underpin it, so the old lais can provide a fruitful and above all enjoyable means of approach to cleansing the organs of inner perception.

ANONYMOUS LAIS

·I·

Graelent

THE LAIS we give in this section of the book were first assembled in a critical edition entitled *Les Lais anonymes des XII et XIII siécles* by Prudence Mary O'Hara Tobin (Droz, Geneva, 1976). Our rendering them into English, whilst faithful to the original text, seeks to give something of the atmosphere of a jongleur's oral delivery rather than a close academic translation of Old French.

This first lai, *Graelent*, provides a classic example of the close association of a faery with water, particularly a spring or fountain, and also trees and woods and hunting in one form or another – often of a hind or stag, sometimes a boar, and almost invariably white, the faery colour.

The faery at the fountain, sometimes accompanied by two companions, seems to be very much in control even if at first appearing not to be so. Although the meeting with a mortal seems to be by chance, it generally turns out to have been foreseen or even arranged by the faery. For we often find that she knows the mortal wanderer's name, is more than ready to take him on as a lover, and arranges the meeting at a time when the mortal is particularly vulnerable, distressed or disenchanted with the human world in some way.

All these factors appear in *Graelent*. He has been forced into poverty by the machinations of the queen – but the faery knows his name and his impoverished circumstances, so we may assume that she has set up the whole scenario of being found naked bathing at the spring to which Graelent has been led by the white hind. So much for her false modesty and ready acceptance of being violated by the hero – which takes place after a feisty and flirtatious exchange.

It is along the lines of classical faery/human liaisons in that having become his lover there is nonetheless a prohibition or *geiss* attached to it. In this case that he must never reveal the association to anyone else. Even though she cannot be seen by anyone else, strict secrecy must be preserved, which of course he fails in the end to observe. The result is disaster for him. The faery withdraws her love and her presence, leaving him in a particularly dire and life threatening situation.

However, a happy ending of sorts is contrived in that she appears to relent and turns up at the last minute – if only to prove that she is more beautiful than the queen – and thus saves his life and restores his freedom. But a certain implacability of the faery world becomes evident when she still refuses to acknowledge him. She returns to the Otherworld beyond a river which he is unable to cross despite his desperate attempts. He is only saved at the last through the intercession of the faery's two companions. Even so, he is never seen in the human world again – having been taken off to Faeryland – to the continued distress of the horse he left behind him.

There are several hints of ancient traditions contained in this lai, particularly to do with the queen. She is obviously not one to be slow in coming forward when she conceives a lust for one of her subjects, and her thwarted love can easily turn into hate, and not just subjectively held either, as she vindictively seeks his impoverishment.

This is exacerbated by the pride she feels in being hailed the most beautiful woman in the land in a strange and somewhat barbaric ceremony where she is exhibited annually before all the barons, having taken off her mantle (and anything else one may wonder) for the purpose. And in which Graelent refuses to join in the accustomed adulation.

One also finds the issue of a beauty contest involving the queen in Chrétien de Troyes' first Arthurian romance *Erec et Enide* (or its Welsh version *Geraint and Enide* or *The Lady of the Fountain*) wherein Erec finds a faery bride who eventually leads him into the Otherworld. (cf. *The Faery Gates of Avalon* by Gareth Knight, R.J. Stewart Books, 2008).

Another faery issue that is somewhat glossed over in the lai is where the host's daughter in Graelent's lodging house invites him to dine alone with her and provides him with horse and saddle. This is similar to the traditional theme of the Hospitable Host and his daughter who entertain a questing hero, and/or provide him with horse and/or arms, on the bounds of the Otherworld.

We are fortunate in having the story of Graelent closely followed by one collected by Marie de France under the name *Lanval*. It is interesting to compare the two, to see how Marie tends to play down the marvels whilst at the same time presenting a more coherent and well connected literary work. There are a number of crudities in *Graelent* which any copy writer (whether 12th century or 21st century) would have corrected had the story been produced as a work of literature rather than the script for impromptu entertainment. Such confusions are minor – relating to the types of horse that Graelent has, and even if he has any at all when he is impoverished. We will however reserve such comparisons until we come to relate the *Lanval* of Marie de France in Part 3.

LET ME TELL YOU the tale of Graelent, just as I learned it. It is good to hear these stories even without the music.

Graelent was born of Breton parents, noble and well endowed. He was handsome and loyal of heart, and they called him Graelent the Great. When the king who reigned in Brittany went to war he called all his knights about him and for certain Graelent was there because he was such a fine knight. The king cherished and honoured him and Graelent took part in many tourneys and jousts in which he beat all his adversaries.

The queen heard about this and all the praise that was heaped on him, became intrigued and called her chamberlain.

"Tell me all you know about this knight Graelent," she said. "Does he have admirers everywhere?"

"Lady," he replied, "he is so brave and true that he is loved by everyone."

"I would have him love me," she said, "I feel strangely drawn to him. Tell him to come to me and I will offer him my love."

"That would be a most precious gift," said the chamberlain, "and it would be a wonder if he were not overjoyed! There is no man between here and Troyes abbey who could contain himself at the thought of your love."

The chamberlain left and went to Graelent's lodgings, greeted him warmly and gave him the message from the queen:

"She wants to see you privately, and now!"

"Go on ahead, my friend, and I will follow," replied the knight.

The chamberlain went off while Graelent got himself ready, mounted his iron grey steed and took a fellow knight for company. The two arrived at the castle, dismounted in the great hall, passed before the king's chambers and entered those of the queen.

When she saw them, she called Graelent to her with every sign of honour and affection. She took him in her arms, held him close, and made him sit beside her. As she spoke she gazed upon his face and body and entertained him courteously. He responded simply, though said nothing to encourage her.

The queen was cautious at first, reluctant to demand his affection outright. But the desire she felt for him made her bold. She enquired if he had a lover. If his heart was taken elsewhere. For he certainly deserved to be loved.

"Lady", he said, "I love no one for it is no easy game to be faithful in love. Whoever does must have great merit. Hundreds talk of love who do not know its snares and that it must be a loyal affection. By their rage, their folly, their laziness, their laxity, their lies, they wrong love in a thousand ways. Love demands honesty in thought and word and deed. If one of the lovers is loyal and the other jealous or false, then love is spoiled and cannot last for long. Love needs but one companion, it is only sincere between two people united in body and soul; otherwise it has no value. Cicero, who spoke of friendship said very strongly in his book that whatever one lover wants, the other wishes too, and their agreement is perfect. If she expresses a wish and he agrees, their bond is strong. But if one contradicts the other, it is no longer love but harshness. One can easily find love, but to keep it needs wisdom, tenderness, nobility of soul, moderation: love cannot stand a grave fault. One must promise fidelity and respect that promise. And so I dare not care to think of it."

The queen sat through these bookish words of Graelent and would have liked to stop him talking there and then. Now she spoke in turn – and frankly bared her feelings.

"Dear Graelent," she said, "I love you deeply. I have only ever loved my husband, but I love you sincerely too. So be my love, and I will be yours."

"Thank you, lady," he replied, "but it cannot be so, for I am a servant of the king. I have promised him loyalty and fidelity, and to defend his life and honour. He will never be put to shame by me."

With that he abruptly rose and left.

When he had gone the queen began to sigh, desolate and not knowing what to do. But she did not intend to renounce him for all that. Many times after she prayed him, sent messages, offered him rich presents but he repulsed them all.

Not being able to attain her ends she began to hate him, and put him on bad terms with her husband by frequent slanders. So much so, that when the king next went to war, Graelent was left behind. He spent little, for little now remained for him. He depended on the king for his pay, but the king now made him wait for it, and thanks to the manoeuvres of the queen of late the king had given him nothing. Condemned to poverty, what could Graelent do? There remained for him nothing but to pawn his charger, and then, no longer having a war horse, he could not seek another master.

Graelent sought help from no one. It was May, when the days are long. His host had risen early and gone with his wife to dine with another townsman. The knight was left alone, with no one to keep him company, apart from the daughter of the house, a very friendly girl.

When time for dinner arrived, she came to find the knight and invited him to eat with her. But he felt no pleasure in that. He called his squire and told him to bring him a hunting horse and saddle it as he wished to go riding.

"You no longer have a saddle," the squire replied.

"I can lend you a saddle my friend," said the maiden, "and a good bridle too."

The squire brought the horse, saddled it and Graelent mounted and rode off through the town. He was dressed in an old leather coat that he had worn for a very long time. Townsfolk who saw him did not refrain from jokes and mockery; as is the weakness of common people. They do not know their manners, for all of them lack courtesy.

Beyond the town were wide orchards, and then a great forest through which a river flowed. Graelent strayed there, pensive, doleful and alone.

But he had hardly entered the wood when in a dense thicket he saw a hind, completely white, whiter than snow on a winter branch, which bounded off at the sight of him. He shouted out and spurred his horse, and although he could not gain on it he followed close behind.

It led him to a clearing in which a spring of water gushed beautiful and clear. A maiden was bathing there, attended by two others who stood to one side. She had taken off her clothes, which were scattered under the trees.

Seeing her naked Graelent quickly approached, no longer caring about the hind. She was lithe, slender and attractive, her white skin freshly coloured, and she had laughing eyes in a pretty face. He thought he had never seen anyone so beautiful in all the world.

He let her go on bathing peacefully, intent on seizing her clothes. The other two maidens were frightened and ran some way off on seeing the knight, but the one in the water called out in anger.

"Graelent, leave my clothes! You have no right to keep me naked! Give me at least my shift! You can have the cloak – you can get a good price for it in the market!"

Graelent answered hotly "I am not a merchant's son, or a tradesman to peddle women's clothes. If your cloak were worth three castles I would not take it. But if you want to get dressed, come out of the water and talk to me."

"No I will not!" she said. "For you will only carry me off. And I don't care what you say – I have nothing in common with the likes of you."

"So be it," he replied. "I will keep your clothes until you do come out. My word, your body is lovely."

When she saw that he would not return her clothes, she asked him to promise to do her no harm. Graelent promised and tossed her the chemise. As she came out of the water he held the cloak before her and gallantly threw it over her shoulders. Then he took her by the hand, led her away from the other maidens and asked if she would be his lover.

"Graelent," she replied, "you ask too much. You lack wisdom. I am astonished you dare use that language to me. Do not be so impetuous, it could cost you dear. No woman of my lineage would consort with a man of your rank."

Graelent thought her very proud and saw his prayer was in vain, that she would not willingly accord him his pleasure. But he did not intend to leave things like that. He dragged her off into a deeper part of the woods and there he had his way with her.

Having satisfied his desire, he asked her gently not to hold it against him, but to be generous and reasonable. If she would give him her love freely, he would love her faithfully in return and never leave her.

The maiden paid attention to Graelent's words, and could see he was a good knight, brave and generous, and who knew what he wanted. She would never have a lover so sure. So she agreed to be his lover and sealed it with a tender kiss.

"Graelent," she said, "you took me by surprise, I will love you sincerely, but I forbid you one thing. Never by a single word allow our love to be known. I will give you an abundance of money and clothes, gold and silver, and our love together will be perfect. Night and day I will lie with you, you will feel me come and go at your side. You can speak to me, laugh with me, but not a single one of your companions must see me or know who I am.

"I know you are faithful Graelent, valiant, courteous and handsome. It was for you that I came to play at the fountain, but because of you I know I may suffer great pain if you do not take care. Beware of boasting of me indiscreetly, or you will lose me. You will need, my love, to stay near here for a year, for I love this place; but you can go away for two whole months at a time on condition that you return. Now go, it is three in the afternoon. I will send you my messenger who will let you know my will." And as Graelent took leave of her, she took him in her arms and covered him with kisses.

He arrived at his lodgings, dismounted, entered his room alone and went to the window, thinking of his adventure. As he looked toward the forest he saw a squire coming on a palfrey, leading a great war horse, who did not stop until he arrived at Graelent's lodging. Graelent ran down to meet him, asked where he came from, his name and who he was.

"Sir," he said, "have no doubt, I am your lover's messenger. By me she sends you this destrier, and wishes me to stay with you. I will pay your debts and take care of your lodging."

Graelent was delighted at this news, and heartily embraced the young man as he received from him the finest, most agile and fastest charger in the world. He put it in the stables himself, along with the messenger's horse. Meanwhile the young man unloaded his trunk, carried it to Graelent's room, opened it, and took out a great coverlet, made of fine cloth on one side and embroidered silk on the other. He put it on Graelent's bed, along with gold and silver, and rich stuffs to clothe his master. Then he called the host, gave him money in abundance, declaring that as his master was quit of his debts and the price of his lodging completely paid, that he now provide abundant food. And if he knew of any knight in town in need of a restful place to stay, to bring him back with him.

The host was wise and of good breeding for a townsman. He had a copious meal prepared and searched the town for any unfortunate knights, prisoners or needy crusaders. He brought them back to the house where Graelent treated them with honour. They passed the evening in music and song and many pleasant diversions. Graelent, in good humour and sumptuous attire, gave generously to the harpers, the prisoners and the musicians. And each townsman who had made him a loan was laden with gifts and other considerations of the kind one sees generally only from a lord.

Thus was Graelent content. All he saw gave him pleasure. He saw his lover come and go, laughed and played with her, and at night felt her close by his side. How could he not be happy? He often travelled to other countries and was honoured by other knights, and there was no tourney where he did not carry off the prize. Graelent now lived a pleasant life and his lover was a source of joy to him. If all had lasted longer, he could have asked for nothing more. Thus he lived for a whole year.

Each year at Pentecost the king proclaimed a feast for all the barons who held land from him. After the meal, he had the queen stand on a high platform, when she would take off her cloak as he asked them all; "My lord barons, what do you say? Is there anywhere on earth any lady, maiden, or servant girl more beautiful than the queen?"

Each had to make his praises and affirm he knew none so beautiful, whether servants, ladies or maidens. All without exception praised her beauty, except Graelent who remained silent. He smiled to himself, thinking in his heart of his lover. He took the others for fools who shouted cries of admiration in praise of the queen, and he bowed his head and lowered his gaze.

The queen saw this, and complained to her husband the king.

"See, sire, what dishonour! Not a single one of your barons has failed to praise me, apart from Graelent, who mocks me. I have suspected for long that he detested me, but now he openly shows nothing but contempt."

The king called Graelent before him, and in the name of the faith that Graelent owed to him as his vassal, demanded to know why he had lowered his head and smiled.

"Sire," replied Graelent, "pray hear me. Never has a man of your quality acted so foolishly. You exhibit your wife and there is not a single baron that you do not require to praise her – to claim there is no one in the world her equal! Ah well, I will give you some news: I know a lady much more beautiful."

At these words, the king was dismayed and forced him to swear under oath that he knew one who was more attractive than the queen.

"Oh yes," Graelent replied, "and worth thirty of her too!"

The queen was deeply wounded by this. She implored her husband to oblige the knight to bring forth the woman he praised and vaunted so much.

"Let there be a test between the two of us," she said. "If she is as beautiful, then let him be quit; but if not, give me justice for this outrage and slander."

The king ordered that Graelent be seized. "You will have no affection or peace on my part," he declared, "nor leave prison until you show us the one you have so praised."

Graelent was put under heavy guard and realised he had spoken foolishly and might even have lost his lover. Filled with concern and regret he begged a delay from the king, who allowed him until the next year, to be present at the feast and bring with him the one whom he had so praised. If she was truly as beautiful as the queen his life would be spared. But if she failed to come, or were judged less beautiful, Graelent would be at the mercy of the king – and knew well the consequences.

Graelent left the court sad and returned to his lodging. He looked for the chamberlain who had been provided by his lover, but could not find him anywhere. Greatly embarrassed, he retired alone to his room to implore the pity of his lover. But all was in vain. He could not even speak to her.

For a whole year, with death in his soul, he received no consolation from her. Graelent fell into sadness, without rest night or day. Since he had lost his lover he attached no value to life. Before the year was up, he was so beaten down he had no more strength to resist. Those who saw him said it was a marvel he had survived so long. On the appointed day, the king held his feast with all the barons in attendance. Graelent was brought into their presence and asked where his lover was.

"Sire," he said, "I do not know. I have been unable to find her. Do with me as you will."

"Sir Graelent," replied the king, "your offence has been considered. You have both offended the queen and denied the wisdom of my barons. But you will slander no one else after you have left our hands.

"Lords," he continued in a loud voice, "I pray you do not delay in passing your judgement. You know what Graelent said in your presence. He has covered the queen in shame and my court as well. He does not love me with a true affection if he dishonours my wife. If anyone even kicked your dog you would know he did not love you well."

The men of the court retired and met for their verdict but remained for some time in silence, perplexed, for they did not want to pass severe judgment on such a knight. But before any of them could say a word or make a proposal, a young man appeared. He asked them to wait a little: two maidens, he said, would soon arrive at the court, the most beautiful in the kingdom. They had come to aid the knight, and with God's help, would deliver him.

The barons willingly waited, and before long the maidens arrived, slender and of great beauty, in sumptuous clothes, decorated with ermine. Dismounting from their palfreys, which they gave to their valets to hold, they entered the hall and walked toward the king.

"Sire," said one, "pray give heed. Our lady prays you delay this trial a little and not yet pass judgment. She is coming to speak with you and to deliver the knight." At this message the queen was overcome with embarrassment.

A little later, two more maidens, even more beautiful, with complexions clear and radiant, presented themselves before the king, and prayed that he await the arrival of their lady. Everyone who looked upon them was astonished by their beauty: there were thus ladies as beautiful as the queen!

But when their lady, their mistress appeared, the whole court had nothing but eyes for her. She was of a rare beauty: a stance full of sweetness, beautiful eyes, a fine face, and elegant hair; she could not be faulted in any way. All looked at her in stupefaction. She was richly dressed in brilliant purple, finely embroidered with gold, and her cloak was worth a castle. She rode a fine and beautiful palfrey, the bridle, saddle and harness worth at least a thousand pounds of gold. Everyone craned to see her, admire her face and figure, her manners, her whole bearing. She arrived at a lively pace on horseback before the king. No one dreamed of criticizing her for that. She dismounted before him, without releasing her palfrey, and courteously addressed the king.

"Sire," she said, "take heed, and you, sir barons, as well. Listen to what I have to say. You know that Graelent, at the great assembly when you last exhibited the queen, said that he knew one more beautiful: everyone knows he said that. It is true he was wrong to speak so and to annoy his king. But on the other hand he was right; no woman is such a beauty that no other can be more so. Look then! May your judgement be fair. And then, thanks to me, let Graelent be released and declared innocent."

There was no one, great or small, not convinced that Graelent had produced a lady whose beauty excelled that of the queen. The king in person gave his judgement before the court and pronounced Graelent acquitted. During which time, Graelent had his white horse brought, intending to leave with her.

When she heard the verdict of the court, she took leave of the king, remounted her horse and left the hall, accompanied by her maidens. Graelent took to saddle and followed her through the town, imploring her forgiveness, but she did not answer a word.

When they arrived at the forest and came to the bank of the river, its water pure and beautiful, the damsel plunged straight into it. But when Graelent tried to follow she cried out to him: "Fly, Graelent, do not come in or you will drown!"

He took no notice but dashed into the water. It closed over his head and only after some time did he regain the surface. She seized his horse by the reins, pulled him back to the bank, and said again he could not cross the river, no matter how he tried.

She entered the water again, but he could not bear to see her leave him. He leaped into the river after her; and this time the current took him, depriving him of his horse.

He was on the point of drowning when the damsel's maidens cried:

"Lady, by God, have pity on your friend! He is drowning! Alas! Cursed be the day when you first spoke to him and granted him your love! See, the current is taking him. Oh lady, pull him from danger or he will die! How in your heart can you let him suffer? You are too hard on him. Help him, go to his aid, or his death will be on your hands."

The damsel had pity as she listened to their cries. Quickly she turned back to the river, seized her lover round the waist and held him close to her. Once on the bank, she removed his sodden clothes, covered him with her cloak and took him with her into her own country.

Some say that Graelent is still living. His destrier, who came through it all, showed a great sadness for his master; it returned to the bank, and pined for him night or day. It pawed the ground with its hooves, neighing loudly; and could be heard through the whole country. Some tried to take it and keep it, but none of them could. It ran off and no one could trap or bridle it. A long time after, it was said, each year at the time that Graelent disappeared, its cries could be heard for the master it had lost.

The story of the faithful destrier and that of the knight who went away with his lover was told throughout Brittany. The Bretons made a lai of it and called it the Lai of Graelent the Dead.

Guingamor

THE STORY in this lai is similar to *Graelent* but less crudely put together and has significant variations. There is problem with a queen again, although presented in a more subtle fashion, and with the minor variant of it being a boar that the hero hunts, combining faery revelation with a test of courageous knighthood.

The strange boar hunt, which is quite protracted and almost surreal in parts, as the beast and the pursuing bratchet keep appearing and disappearing, emphasises something of a quest and test as a preliminary to meeting the faery. Perhaps it is on the strength of this test that he finds himself confronted first with the magnificent faery palace as a preliminary to meeting the mistress of it in the conventional scenario of the naked faery in a pool with her clothing spread around in disarray.

He is then treated right royally and strikes up a bargain with the faery powers, although it soon becomes obvious that he may never be able to return to the human world. There is no direct prohibition to be observed here, apart from a warning that involves the difference in time scale between the two worlds. Three days in the Otherworld turns out to be three hundred years in human terms.

Even so when Guingamor returns, against all advice, he need not have fallen into trouble if he had observed the faery's warning about eating or drinking whilst in the human realm. There is a certain faery traditional touch in that the fruit that tempts him in the end are wild apples – for apples and orchards are continual features in tales of faery, the traditional Avalon being the island of apples.

As in Graelent it appears that Guingamor is eventually rescued by the faeries at the last moment but only at the cost of disappearing for ever into the Otherworld.

We thus have an instance in both these lais of what Laurence Harf-Lancner categorises as a "morganatic" faery – one who takes the hero off into her own world rather than occupy the human world in the guise of a human woman, which is called a "melusinian" faery, after the example of Melusine of Lusignan.

 WILL TELL YOU a story told in a lai. And do not think it never happened, for it is the honest truth and is called the Lai of Guingamor.

There was once a king who ruled in Brittany, a noble lord but whose name I forget. He had a wise and courteous nephew called Guingamor, a brave knight full of good sense. The king held him in great affection on account of his valour and beauty, and not having any children, decided to make his nephew his heir. Guingamor deserved this honour, being large in promise and gifts, and was famed for his generosity and wisdom and for treating his knights, servers and squires honourably.

One day the king went hunting in the forest. But that day his nephew had been bled and felt a little unwell because of it. Not wanting to go to the woods, he decided to rest at home with a few companions, after which he went to the castle where he was greeted warmly by the seneschal. After some talk they sat down to play a game of chess.

As they were playing, the queen, who was slender, attractive and beautiful, came out of her chamber on her way to chapel and paused in the doorway. She stood there for some time, not taking another step, at the sight of the knights playing chess. Guingamor seemed handsome to her in body, face and dress, seated against a window, where a ray of sunlight shone on his face, flooding it with light and giving him a striking air. The queen was quite overcome.

She retraced her steps and called a servant.

"Go," she said, "to the knight seated over there at chess, Guingamor, the king's nephew, and tell him to come to me."

The servant approached the knight, saluted him on behalf of her mistress and prayed him to go and speak with her. Guingamor left the game and went with the servant. The queen invited him to sit by her. He did not understand why she accorded him so fine a welcome and the queen was the first to speak.

"Guingamor, you are valiant, proud, courteous and becoming; and a fine adventure awaits you. You could be loved in very high places you know. In fact I know there is one who loves you. She is both courtly and beautiful, and there is no other maiden in the kingdom to match her. She loves you madly and desires to have you as her lover."

"Lady," replied the knight, "I cannot understand how I can be deeply loved by a lady whom I do not know, have not seen, and never met. I have not heard tell of her, and anyway for the present I am not concerned about love."

"My friend," said the queen, "do not be so shy. It is I who love you so much, and I will not accept a refusal. I love you with all my heart and will do so for all my life."

The knight was perplexed but replied as sensibly as he could: "I know very well, my lady, that I must love you; for you are the wife of my lord the king, and I owe you respect as the wife of my lord."

"I do not speak of love of that sort," she replied. "I want you to love me as your paramour. You are handsome and I am beautiful; so love me in return and we can have much pleasure together." She drew closer and kissed him.

Guingamor now realised the love she wished for and blushed for shame. In confusion he rose to leave the chamber. She tried to restrain him, and seized his cloak so fiercely that she pulled it from his back. He left without his cloak and, very troubled, sat down again at the chess board, so disconcerted that he forgot his cloak, and in this state resumed the game.

The queen now became very anxious. After her proposal and Guingamor's refusal, she feared he would denounce her to the king. She called her servant, gave her the cloak and told her to take it to Guingamor. The servant replaced it on his shoulders, but he was so anxious, plunged in thought that he did not even notice her. The maiden then returned.

The queen remained apprehensive until evening. When the king returned from the hunt he sat down to eat with his companions. They had had a good day and all were in good humour. After the meal there were games and laughter, and the hunters told of their exploits, each telling what he had done, who had missed his mark, and who had fared well.

Guingamor now regretted not having taken part in the hunt. He remained still and quiet, and the queen watched him. Then in order to be rid of him she conceived a plan that would give pleasure to no one.

Turning toward the knight she said: "I have heard much praise of
you and tales of your adventures, but of all those I see here, not one of
them I think, even if promised a thousand pounds in gold, would be
brave enough to sound the horn and hunt the white boar in the forest.
Whoever could do that would really deserve renown."

All the knights were silent, for all feared to take on such a test, and
Guingamor understood very well that the challenge was addressed to
him. All remained pensive and silent and the first to respond was the
king: "Lady, we have often heard tell of that adventure in the forest,
but know that I detest hearing it spoken – by anyone. No man who has
gone to hunt that beast has ever returned. The country is dangerous
with a river full of perils. I have suffered heavy losses, ten knights, the
best in my country, who have gone to hunt that boar."

When the meeting dispersed each one returned to his lodging and
the king to his bed. But Guingamor could not forget what he had
heard. He entered the king's chamber and knelt before him.

"Sire," he said, "I pray that you grant me something of which I have
great need. And although I have not told you what it is, I pray you will
not refuse me."

"Dear nephew," said the king, "I will grant you anything that pleases
you. So tell me, do not be afraid to ask. You shall have whatever you
wish."

The knight thanked him gratefully, and told him he wanted to
hunt the white boar. For which he asked to borrow his bloodhound,
his bratchet and his hunting horse, and also prayed the king to lend
him his pack of hounds for the day.

The king was dismayed and knew not what to do. He wanted to
go back on his word and have Guingamor renounce his request. He
would rather have paid his weight in gold than let him go hunting the
white boar, for he knew he might never return, along with his dogs
and his hunting horse – which he treasured above all else in the world.
He might never see any of them again. All would be lost and he left
inconsolable.

"Sire," replied Guingamor, "in the name of the loyalty I owe you,
I will not renounce the hunt at any price. If you gave me the whole
world, tomorrow I would still go to hunt the boar. If you do not wish
to lend me the bratchet that you love so much, or the hunting horse,
the blood hound and the hunting pack, I will take my own."

The queen overheard all this and was surprised, but it gave her great relief. She prayed the king to consent to the knight's wishes, counting thus to be rid of him and never to be seen at court again. Guingamor took his leave and returned to his lodging joyfully, but he did not sleep a wink all night.

When morning came, he prepared for the hunt and said farewell to his companions. Everyone at the palace was concerned for him. Had they been able, they would have turned him away from this hunt by whatever means they could. Guingamor went for the horse that, the evening before, he had borrowed from the king, taking also the bratchet, the fine horn, that he would not have left behind for its weight in gold, and two fine packs of hounds of the king – not forgetting the bloodhound.

The king provided an escort and all the townspeople, merchants, journeymen, as well as the courtiers turned out, deeply affected, with dolorous lamentations. The ladies especially could not hide their anguish.

The huntsmen arrived at the little wood near the city to open up the way, led by the bloodhound. They searched for some trace of the boar, which usually foraged in this area, and finally found it in a dense thicket. They unleashed the bloodhound, and its baying raised the boar which rushed from the bushes.

Guingamor sounded his horn, held back one pack of hounds near the forest and advanced with the other. At the start of the chase, quitting the bushes, the boar twisted and turned every way along the edge of the woods. The hounds tracked it with great baying until they were exhausted. Guingamor then released the second pack and continued to sound his horn, the pack closing in on the game so it could not return to the bushes. Thus it threw itself into the forest. Guingamor followed it, carrying before him the bratchet he had borrowed from the king.

Those who escorted him, the king, his knights and the people from the town, had stopped at the edge of the forest. The king forbade them to go any further. They stayed there as long as they could, hearing the distant sound of the horn and the baying of the hounds. Then they turned back and commended the soul of Guingamor to God.

The boar ran on, tiring out the rest of the hounds, so Guingamor unleashed the bratchet and set it to the ground. The dog ran after the beast but the knight had hardly the strength to sound his horn. The barking of the dog encouraged him, until he lost it from view, and then could no longer even hear the sound of dog or boar. Distraught and with death in his soul at the thought of having lost the dog his uncle loved so much, he wandered on through the deepest part of the forest and finally stopped at a lofty mound.

The weather was fine on this beautiful day and birds were singing on all sides, but he paid them no attention. Then he heard the dog baying far away. He began to sound his horn, anxious to see it again. Then in a clearing of beech trees he saw the boar rush through, pursued by the dog in the direction of the moor. He spurred his horse with vigour, and rejoiced that he might now be able to take the boar and return home safe and sound. Then they would speak of him for ever and he would be of great renown.

Joyously, he put the horn to his mouth and blew; the horn gave forth a marvellous sound. The boar passed before him again, with the dog still close behind. Guingamor spurred after them, out of the forest and across the moor, famous for adventures, through which ran a perilous river. Straight across he rode and on towards a flowery meadow. There he thought he might catch up with the boar, but suddenly saw before him the walls of a beautiful palace built of green marble.

At its entrance was a tower that at first sight seemed like silver, it reflected the light with a marvellous brightness. The doors were of ivory, with gold engraving, but had no locks nor bolts. Seeing the great door open and the entrance unmanned, Guingamor decided to go in. He would look around, he thought, for a responsible man or guardian of the place and ask him who was its lord, for he had never seen anything so rich and wonderful. He thought he could find his boar again if he did not stay long, for he felt it must be nearly exhausted.

Thus he entered the gates on horseback and stopped in the middle of the palace to look all around. But he found nothing, although all was of fine gold inset with stones of paradise. What seemed most strange was to find no man nor woman. Anyhow, he was glad to have found a wonder he could tell to all back at court.

He came out quickly and went to the bank of the river. He could now see no trace of his boar. It seemed he had lost it, and the dog as well, and felt much ashamed.

"In faith," he said, "I have been well caught out! I should be taken for a fool to have wasted all my efforts just to admire a house! If I have lost the king's dog and let the boar escape, it is the end of my joy and reputation. There is now nothing left but to return home."

Pensively, he made his way to the heights of the forest and listened for the cry of the dog. As he listened, he heard it again far off, as well as the boar. He sounded his horn once more and chased off to meet them. Suddenly the boar passed right before him, and Guingamor set out to pursue it, his cries exciting the dog.

As he reached the end of the moor he came upon a spring, under a leafy olive tree, green, flowering and luxuriant. The water was clear and beautiful, the gravel beneath like gold and silver. A maiden was bathing there, while another combed her hair and washed her feet and hands. She had a beautiful body, slim and well proportioned. He had never seen anything so beautiful in the world, neither lily, nor rose, as this naked maid.

As soon as Guingamor saw her, struck by her beauty, he pulled up his horse. Her clothes were under a great tree and he quickly rode across to hide them high in the crook of an oak. When he had taken the boar, he said to himself, he would return to the maiden, who could not go far if she was totally naked.

But she saw what he was at, and called to him fiercely: "Guingamor, do not touch my clothes! May God forbid that you live to tell your fellow knights you committed such an outrage – to steal the clothes of a maiden in the heart of the forest! But have no fear, I will show you where I live. You have been working hard all day, and with no great result."

Guingamor went towards her, and brought her clothes. He thanked her for her offer but said he could not accept her hospitality as he had lost the boar as well as his dog.

"My friend," replied the damsel, "no one in the world could find them without my help, whatever their efforts. So give up your foolish enterprise and come with me. I promise I will deliver the boar to you within three days, along with the bratchet, to take back to your country."

The maiden dressed and her companion brought a mule richly harnessed, well saddled, with a palfrey for herself that would have been the envy of any count or king. Guingamor followed the maiden, and having helped her into the saddle, mounted his horse and took the reins. He gazed at her many times, joyous at heart, and found her beauty so striking he hoped she loved him in return. Fixing her with his eyes he prayed that she grant him her love. Never before had he lost his heart to a woman or ever dreamed of love.

She was wise and compliant and replied she would willingly love him, which filled the knight with joy. Assured of her love, he pulled her to him and embraced her.

Going before, her servant spurred on to arrive at the palace where Guingamor had been, to have it sumptuously decorated. She called upon the knights therein to mount, and brought them to meet their lady and to honour the friend that she brought. It was a fine company. There were three hundred or more, all dressed in surcoats of silk embroidered with gold, and each one brought his lady with him. There were young people carrying fine hawks, and others from the palace who had been playing trictrac or chess.

When Guingamor arrived, he saw among them knights from his own country, boar hunters whom he thought had been lost. All stood up in his presence, saluted him with joy and Guingamor embraced them. He had comfortable lodging that night with succulent meats in abundance, many amusements and music of harps and vielles with songs by young men and maidens. He marvelled at all this noble and lavish beauty. He had no intention to stay more than two days and to leave on the third, with the bratchet and boar, to let his uncle know his marvellous adventure. After which he would return to his lover.

But it turned out very much otherwise. He had stayed there for three hundred years! The king was dead, as well as those of his house and his lineage, and the towns that Guingamor had known were now in ruins or destroyed. But Guingamor said he wished to return to his country, and prayed his lover to bring him his bratchet and the boar.

"Friend," she said, "you can have them if you wish, but your departure is foolish; you have been here for three hundred years. Your uncle and his people are dead, you have no more friends or relations. And there will be no man old enough to answer your questions, whatever they may be."

"Lady," he said, "I cannot believe that is true. But if it is I will return here quickly, I promise you."

"Well I will warn you," she said, "once you have crossed the river to return to your country, do not drink or eat anything, no matter how great your hunger or thirst, or you will be struck by a spell."

She had his horse brought and the body of the great boar, and gave him his dog on a leash. He took the boar's head, not wanting to carry more, mounted his horse and rode off. His lover accompanied him as far as the river, which he crossed in a boat, commended himself to God, and left.

The knight rode on till midday before reaching the end of the forest. What he saw there was so wild and unkempt that he did not recognise it. Far off, on his left, he heard a charcoal burner cutting trees with his axe, to make a fire. He spurred his horse in that direction, saluted the man and asked him where was the king, his uncle, and in which castle he was staying.

"In faith, sir," replied the charcoal burner, "I know nothing about that! The king you speak of has been dead, so far as I know, for more than three hundred years, along with his court and his people. As for the castle you mention, it has for a long time been in ruins. There are still a few old people who talk about that king and his nephew, who was so brave but went hunting in the forest and was never seen again."

Hearing these words, Guingamor was filled with immense pity for the king and all he had lost.

"Give heed to what I say," he said to the charcoal burner, "and I will tell you my story. It was I who went on that hunt after the great white boar."

He told him about the palace he had found, how he had entered it, about the maiden he met and had stayed with for two whole days, and when he left had given him his dog and the head of the boar. He gave the boar's head to the charcoal burner, and told him to keep it until he returned and use it to prove his story to the people of the country. The poor man thanked him and Guingamor took his leave and departed.

It was well into the afternoon, and as evening approached the knight was taken with such great hunger that he thought he would go mad. At the side of the way he came upon a tree full of wild apples. He approached, and took three to eat them.

Unfortunate for him that he forgot the advice of his lover. Hardly had he tasted one than he became old and decrepit, so feeble that he fell from his horse and could move neither hand nor foot. In a weak voice, when he had recovered the use of speech, he started to lament.

The charcoal burner, who had followed, saw him and thought he would never live until evening. But as he was about to go for aid two damsels arrived, well and richly dressed. They dismounted near Guingamor and blamed the knight in lively terms for having ignored the advice he had so badly observed. Then they took him gently, sat him carefully on his horse, led him to the river and passed across in a boat.

The charcoal burner returned home that night, bearing the head of the boar and told the whole of the adventure, swearing on oath it was true. He gave the head to the king who had it displayed at many feasts. And to perpetuate the memory of the adventure he had a lai composed bearing the name of Guingamor. And thus is it called by the Bretons.

·III·

Désiré

THE COMPLICATED TALE in this lai is located in Scotland and there is also a sort of Christian motif running through the story. The hero is conceived only after intercession from a Christian saint, following a pilgrimage for that very purpose by the hitherto infertile parents, all the way to the shrine of St. Gilles in Provence.

Much then hangs on the role of a hermit in the forest whom Désiré is on the way to visit when he happens upon a faery. Rather as we have seen with Graelent, he is all set to violate her as a matter of course but it turns out that the faery maiden is but the servant of a more powerful faery, and she diverts Désiré's attention with the promise of favours from her even more beautiful faery mistress.

The latter, sitting in her faery bower, on seeing him approach flees into the forest, but after what seems to have been little more than a token flight lies back for the inevitable, and announces her love for him. It is a relationship that lasts for some years, in token of which she gives him a magic ring.

She continues to provide him with great riches although the two never live together, but keep to their own worlds, meeting for assignations in the forest. In the course of time she bears him two children although, surprisingly, and one would think with some difficulty, she does not reveal this to him.

Trouble comes when he eventually does meet up with the hermit, decides to make his confession to him, and includes a mention of his faery lover. This seems to pass off at the time as no great problem but the faery knows all about it and does not like it, even though there has been no formal prohibition or *geiss* laid upon their relationship. As a result the magic ring disappears from Désiré's finger and he loses all contact with his lover.

This leads him to curse the day he ever saw the hermit, along with the whole system of confession, reducing him to great depression and sickness which within a year brings him close to death.

However, the faery appears to relent and turns up at his sick bed to announce that all is forgiven, that she is by no means opposed to the Christian faith and as proof of this agrees to attend mass with him as well as renew their loving relationship.

All does not end here however, for Désiré's son by the faery (possibly in the form of a stag at first) turns up to make the acquaintance of his father, and stays with him for a couple of months before deciding to return to the faery forest. Désiré finds this parting difficult to bear and pursues him, only to lose track and become lost in the forest with night falling. However, he comes upon a dwarf who welcomes and feeds him but who turns out to be treacherous (as dwarves tended to be in medieval romance) and Désiré returns home badly wounded.

He remains at court, in a debilitated condition, until one day his son returns, along with his daughter as well as their faery mother. Their purpose is threefold. The son seeks to be dubbed knight by the king, the daughter to be married, and is indeed so beautiful that the king himself takes her for his queen. Meanwhile the faery desires above all to be made a respectable woman by being wed in church to Désiré. After the ceremony she goes off with him back into the forest and neither of them are ever seen again.

Altogether it is hardly a coherent and limpid account of faery tradition but contains some interesting magical side effects allied with what seems to be a somewhat confused attempt to assert that faery contacts are not necessarily incompatible with religious belief and practice.

NOW BEND MY CARE and effort to tell an adventure which those who lived in that time made into a lai to preserve the memory. It is the lai of Désiré, a young man of great beauty.

There was in Scotland a region called Calatria, near to the White Land on the edge of the great sea, and there the Black Chapel was, very beautiful, on which the crux of this story depends.

There was then a *vavasseur* very well regarded in this country, who held his land as a vassal of the King of Scotland. He had a wife of as great nobility as himself who was full of wisdom and whom he loved passionately. Unhappily they had no children. They suffered much because of this and often asked God in their prayers to have pity on them, and console them with a son or daughter.

One night as they were lying in their bed, the lady said to her spouse:

"Sir, I have heard tell that in Provence, beyond the sea, there are the relics of a famous saint; and ladies go there with their husband. No one, coming from near or far who implores their need goes without an answer to their prayer. They have received from God the grace to give them children. I am very sad at heart, let us cross the sea and go there."

Her husband approved and they prepared for their journey without delay. They crossed the sea and went to St. Gilles and prayed to the saint. They left on an altar a silver statue worth six marks and asked the saint for a son or a daughter. Their prayer made, they returned home, and the lady became pregnant as soon as she entered their house. Her husband was completely happy, and all his relations had never been so joyful.

At the birth of a son, they called him Désiré, for they had for so long waited for this child. St. Gilles had performed a miracle. They raised and pampered their son, who was the object of all their affection and fair in body and face. When he was of an age to leave home they sent him to serve the king where he learned and practised the art of hunting in the forest and of waterfowl. The king also loved and cherished him and dubbed him knight.

As soon as Désiré was made knight he crossed the sea to live in Normandy and attended frequented tourneys in Brittany. He was esteemed by the French and loved by everyone. Knighthood was then an honour, and if a foreign knight left his own country to attain glory at tourneys or at war, he was not given a beating or captured and ransomed by his fellows.

Désiré lived there for ten years before returning, having distinguished himself and acquired renown. When he arrived he was much welcomed by the king who esteemed him for his valour and treated him with high regard, for he was both brave and handsome, and everybody praised him. He only left the king to go back to Calatria when his father invited him to visit his mother.

It was the beginning of summer, and three days after his arrival, he rose one fine morning, richly dressed, as became a knight, with culottes, linen shirt whiter than an April flower, and wearing a green mantle. He put on his spurs and took a good horse that he intended to train. The horse was fine and strong, perfect in body, head and speed, beyond all reproach. Désiré mounted the destrier like the good horseman he was and went down towards the town.

Then, without companions, he rode off toward the White Land. As he gazed on the trees and flowers, and heard the song of the birds, his heart beat more strongly, and a desire rose within him as he entered the forest. Beyond the moor, in a little wood, a holy man had established his hermitage. Désiré had been there often to see him and eat his fruit when, in his childhood, he had ridden out with his father and passed by there. The idea came to him to go to see him again and speak to him, if he could find him.

As he rode towards the chapel, he came upon a maiden dressed in a grey and beautiful shift. Her complexion was white and rose, she was well proportioned and pleasant, and without a headdress her hair blew in the wind, while her feet were naked to dabble in the dew. She held two golden basins in her hands and went towards a spring that bubbled up from under a great tree.

The knight, as any of his kind would have done, seized the young girl and sought to lie with her on the green grass and make love to her. And I am sure he would have succeeded had she not implored his pity.

"Sir Knight, get up from here: you can do much better by not outraging me. Let me tell you something, then think again. I accompany a damsel who is the most beautiful in the world, and I can show her to you. But if I do, take care that she does not escape you, whatever she says. For if you are loved by her, you will lack for nothing.

You will have an abundance of gold and silver, as much as you can wish. Do not think I am lying to you. If she does not please you, I will do all I can to give you pleasure, you can count on me, be sure of that. And I give you my word, that from near or far, I will help you in your every need."

Hearing her speak thus, Désiré let her go, and the girl led him straight to her mistress in a leafy bower. She was lying on a fine bed, the covers made of precious silken stuffs, chequered and strewn with flowers, and before her another maiden was seated.

The one who brought Désiré stopped some distance away. "Look there," she said to him, "in that lodge of leaves, at what I promised you. Have you ever seen such a beautiful face, such beautiful hands, such beautiful arms, a body so alluring in those lace up clothes, more beautiful hair, better adorned, better braided? No creature is her equal. I am now honourably released from you. Advance and fear not. Be valiant and generous."

At these words Désiré let her go and advanced toward the bower. When the maiden saw him, she did not wait, but leaped up and ran from the leafy lodge into the thick of the forest. Without losing sight of her, Désiré followed in pursuit. He was agile, did not lack for effort, and soon caught up with her. Seizing her by the hand he courteously addressed her: "My beauty, tell me, why are you so afraid? I am a knight of this country, and can be your servant and your friend. I would give you all I have to be your love."

The damsel thanked him, curtsied low, and assured him she would not repulse him or reject his offer. She would give him her love and he could make her his mistress. They stayed together for some time and he left her only reluctantly, but as she took her leave of him, she told where he could speak with her and how to find her again.

"Désiré, my love," she said, "go back to Calatria. I give you this gold ring and will tell you this: commit yourself to me with all your being. If not, you will lose the ring and also lose me forever. Try to act well and be scrupulous in my regard. Before having my love, you had great merit. It is not good for a knight, because he loves, to be less valorous." She put the ring on his finger, he embraced her and held her to him, then mounted his horse and returned whence he had come.

From then on he gave much largesse, and went on numerous journeys tirelessly. He distributed more gifts in a single month than the king in half a year. And returned from time to time to the country of his lover whom he cherished. They often spoke together and loved so long that he had a son and a daughter by her. But she said nothing of this so he did not know.

One day the king called him and sent him out of the country to go to a far war. On his return Désiré took leave of the king and went back to his own country, Calatria, where he had been born. The day after his arrival he rose early in the morning, mounted his destrier and rode off to the White Land where he went to find his lover. On the way he happened to pass the abode of the holy hermit, and not knowing when he might pass this way again decided to speak to the him and make his confession.

He opened the door, and entered the chapel.

"Sir," he said, "I wish to make my confession and receive absolution." The hermit agreed and Désiré sat, leaned towards him, and confessed all the sins of which he was sure and certain, together with how he had met his lover for the first time. The hermit gave him his counsel and imposed on him a penance, and when Désiré had received absolution he made the sign of the cross, and returned to his horse.

He leaped into the saddle with the aid of the stirrup and, taking the bridle, looked at the fingers of his hand. The ring was no longer there! Seeing this, he was in despair, overwhelmed to think that he had lost the ring. He left with all speed to go to the place where he hoped to find his lover. And there he stayed all day but without a sight of her.

"Fair friend," he cried out, "where are you? When will you see me? Are you angry with me? If I cannot see you I will die, and never more have any joy or pleasure. Have you taken back the ring you gave me? I know very well you made me lose it. Alas! Unhappy that I am! Where is my fault? I love you before anything. Truly you are acting badly. The hermit confessed me, but at no moment did he say anything bad about you. I simply asked him for forgiveness for my sins. If what I have done is unreasonable, my dear one, do not be angry with me. Impose a penance on me. I will forget all the injunctions, the fasts imposed upon me by the hermit if it gives you pleasure, and I will obey you in everything."

But however much he begged, she refused to speak to him. In despair, he heartily cursed the hermitage and the hermit he had found, the mouth that had spoken to him, and all those who had confessed or would ever confess to him.

Seeing these complaints useless, he resigned himself to return back to Calatria. His suffering was profound, it weighed heavily upon him and soon he fell ill. His great joy had changed to sadness, his song to tears. He languished a whole year and more, and all who saw him so lost said that he was dying.

At the end of a year during which he remained bedridden, hear now what happened to him.

One day his squire and his servants left him to sleep; they wanted to frolic about and dare not awake him. After a long sleep he awoke, was surprised to find himself alone and was angered. While he was so annoyed, his lover came to speak with him. He looked and recognised her, and from the joy he felt he leaned on one elbow on his bed as she addressed him with these words.

"Désiré," she said, "you are unfortunate, at the end of your strength, nearly dead. Why die without a fight? Get hold of yourself, your conduct is senseless. If I have hated you for some time, you certainly deserved it. You spoke of me in confession, an unforgivable fault. Was I a burden on you? Was it so great a sin? I have never been your wife, or your fiancée, nor betrothed to you. You have never taken a wife, have never been committed to another. When you asked to make your confession, I knew that it would mean our separation. What does it serve to avow a sin without the firm resolution to renounce it? Often you have been frightened that I enchanted you! Guard against believing that, I am not of evil origin. When you go to church and hear the mass and pray to God, you will see me at your side to eat the holy bread. You have committed a grave fault against me, but because I have so loved you, I will relent a little on my decision. You can see me again each day, laugh and amuse yourself with me. Give up your sadness, and you will obtain no more by going again to confession."

"Sweet beauty," replied the knight, "thank you. Since you bring me this consolation, I am cured and take courage. Nothing has given me such joy." He embraced her, transported with liveliness as she left.

He was completely cured, delivered of his great torment and comforted by the thoughts of happiness that awaited him. When he went to church to pray, his lover came beside him, she ate the holy bread and made with him the sign of the cross. He spoke with her frequently, and there seemed no evil in it. He journeyed and spent as he once had, before suffering the separation from his lover.

The king still loved him with great affection and did not leave him by day or night. One day they went hunting in the forest, bearing bows and arrows. Beyond the walls of the castle they stopped as they saw near a great tree an enormous stag standing there before them. But they could not kill or wound it. Their arrows fell short to the ground before their eyes. Having shot their quivers full they ran to collect the arrows from where they had fallen; but found none there.

"My God!" said the king to Désiré, "we are enchanted! Our arrows fell here, before our eyes, I am sure of it. Yet we cannot find a single one. This is surely a miracle!"

While they spoke thus, they saw a youth before them, handsome, big, well taken, dressed in a well cut coat of scarlet vermilion. He was marvellously beautiful and striking. His head had beautiful curls, his face well proportioned with fresh colours. And he held the arrows in his hands.

His speech was not that of a countryman. First, he saluted the king, gave him back his arrows and to Désiré his own, and addressed him in a friendly fashion:

"Sir," he said, "you are my father; my mother sent me here. She wants me to be with you, so that I can know and see my family. When you spoke to her for the first time in the land where you conceived me, she gave you a little gold ring. You later lost it, which brought you much grief. I have brought it here with me Sir, put it on your finger."

Désiré immediately recognised the ring, took the young man in his arms and embraced and kissed him a hundred times. The king and all his companions embraced him in their turn, and gave a warm welcome to the boy. Désiré told the king how he had conceived the child, and they took him with them and showered him with affection. Désiré loved and cherished him and would not be far from him by night or day.

After two months had passed the young man rose one morning early, mounted his horse and went to meet his father as he came out of church. As he helped him into his saddle, "Sir," he said, "I am going to take my leave of you. I must return to my mother and can no longer stay."

"Oh, dear son," said Désiré, "by all the saints of God, do not do me to death. I would rather die than have you leave me."

But the young man spurred his horse and left at a great gallop. Désiré, desperate to retain his son whom he feared he now had lost, spurred after him, crying out to him to stop and speak to him. But the boy did not heed him, and continued straight on his way, entering the forest.

Désiré followed him all day. Night fell, and the boy continued his course at full tilt. Désiré chased after him but his horse struck up against a great tree and he was dashed to the ground. He got to his feet and seized his horse but now was fatigued, had lost all trace of his son, and knew not which way to go.

He had hardly advanced far, when looking a little to the right, he saw a fire burning under a large leafy oak. Do you know what he thought on seeing this? That a noble lord had camped here who had hunted during the day, and before hunting next day was passing the night here. Guided by the light of the fire, he rode quickly towards it but found only a dwarf, dressed in silk neatly adjusted, grinding pepper in a mortar to cook on his glowing coals the quarters of an enormous boar.

Désiré advanced and saluted him, but the other did not reply. He left the pepper and the mortar, quickly took the destrier, led it to one side, removed its bridle, detached the saddle and gave it fresh grass. Then he returned to the knight, prepared a bed on the grass of rushes and heather, and covered it with a great embroidered cloth. He made the knight sit but did not say a word, and went back to grinding his pepper.

When he had well mixed it and the meal was ready, he took in his hands two gold basins and attached a serviette to his chin. Désiré recognised the bowls at first sight – they were those that the first damsel had carried when he met her in this land.

He said nothing of this to the dwarf who placed a napkin before him, salt and knives, and two cakes of flour. In a great cup of fine gold the dwarf brought him wine and put the quarters of meat before him in a silver bowl. The knight took a knife and cut a good piece of meat, dipped it in the pepper sauce and offered it to the dwarf who ate it. He then raised the lid of a drinking vessel and offered the dwarf a drink, before drinking himself. He did not eat a piece of meat without giving the dwarf a piece that was just as succulent.

The dwarf found him to be so generous, so fine, so courteous, that he could not resist addressing him a word:

"Sir knight," he said, "you are neither foolish nor ill advised, be welcome here! Although I may be beaten for it, if you wish I will speak to you and transgress the orders I have been given. I am sent to meet you, and to furnish you with a lodge and to serve you."

"Friend," replied the knight, "many thanks for that! I wish all the good possible to whoever sent you here and who has provided this comfort."

"It was your lover," replied the dwarf, "who loves you more than her life."

"My lover, thank God!" said Désiré, "then I lack for nothing!"

"In faith, sir, you are right and I will do all in my power so that you can be with her. If you like to follow me, I will take you to her and you can climb into her bed."

"Friend," said the knight, "lead on. I will follow willingly."

When they had finished their meal, the dwarf led Désiré to the castle where his mistress was. They entered and lit candles that gave forth great clarity. They went as far as a room which had neither door nor window, except one, at the end to the right. In the chamber were two beds, with two damsels lying there, who as far as I know were asleep.

The dwarf gave advice to Désiré as he showed him the room. "Sir, look in there! It is your lover lying there and her sister beside her. Enter, have no fear. You will find a servant who will recognise you, I think, who by the light of a candle stitches a coat for my lady."

Désiré took a run and leaped through the window, feet together, but lost his balance and fell in front of the bed, wounding himself in the side. The whole room resounded with the noise. His lover's sister awoke in fright and cried out in alarm. She called the knights and they entered quickly, armed.

She who was stitching the coat now took the knight by the hand and pulled him outside.

"Sir," she said, "here is the reward I promised you. If you had been taken in that chamber you would have been killed I assure you. May it be, in the name of your generosity, that my kindness be not lost. If you see a day or an occasion to help me, sir, do not forget me."

"No," said he, "good friend."

Guided by the damsel, they came upon the dwarf. She gave him a punch in the chest: "Traitor, rogue," she cried, "why did you betray this generous man? Get out, fly from here!" The dwarf ran off quickly.

Back at the fire. Désiré, pained by his wound, lay on the couch and realised they had played some game with him. When he saw the light of day, he took up his saddle, mounted his horse and returned to his own country.

Badly wounded in the side, he remained for a long time in that state until one day when the king decided to hold his court in a castle in Calatria. He had called at Pentecost for all his neighbours and barons, and many came through loyalty to their lord. Désiré, whom the king loved much, was also present at the feast.

When they had come out of the church, and were seated at table ready to eat, there arrived in the hall a marvellous maiden accompanied by a damsel. Both were richly dressed, their clothes worth 100 marks of silver. They rode white mules and each carried a white hawk.

The king and his entourage marvelled at the sight; they were ideally beautiful of body, face and bearing. With them was a young man, the most handsome in the world. They stopped before the king and the elder maiden saluted him.

"Sire," she said, "give heed to me. I come here bringing these two children. Give arms to this young man and take care of this young damsel; they will be for you a source of honour. The truth is that I am their mother and Désiré their father. You must with good heart watch over these children of so brave a knight and the high lady that I am. I have given very great honour to you today by coming from my country to your court."

"Most gracious one," said the king, "I agree with you. I will do all in my power to do as you ask. But dismount, come and be seated, eat and enjoy yourself with us."

"I cannot do that," said she. "But I ask you to respond to my wishes. Let me marry my lover, for I want to take him with me. Once we are legitimately united, he will pass all the rest of his life with me, without need of confession, penitence or pardon."

The king brought arms to dub the young man knight. He buckled on his sword himself and gave him the accolade. The kings of Moray and of Lothian took part in the feast. As a mark of honour, the first gave him his spurs. Then the king, in the presence of all his people, declared he would marry the damsel himself, and she would be their queen, for he had never seen any so beautiful.

Désiré remained a little far off, impatient to make his lover his wife.

They led them to the church and they were married. On their return from the ceremony, his lady took leave to go back to her country, no longer wishing to prolong her stay.

"Mount your horse, Désiré," she said, "and come with me. Now your son is made knight, you can leave him here, and your daughter who is married. It is a great day for you. Know that they will come to see you when they can." Désiré mounted his horse and departed with his lover and stayed with her, without ever returning, nor ever had any wish to do so.

To perpetuate the memory of this adventure, they made this lai that is called the Lai of Désiré.

·IV·

Tydorel

THE LAI OF Tydorel is interesting because it features a male faery character rather than a female seductress and benefactor. Here again we have, as in Désiré, the situation of a childless couple. However, whereas in Désiré the couple overcame their problem by going on pilgrimage to a Christian saint, in Tydorel the situation is resolved by the direct and unsolicited intervention of the faery world.

The male faery in Tydorel shows all the characteristics of faery in being extremely handsome and in many respects an idealisation of a human knight. But whereas a female faery seduces by means of making herself appear vulnerable, her male counterpart, as revealed here, shows a male characteristic of demonstrating power – even to the point of showing off his magical abilities by galloping under the waters of a great lake, which also of course has the symbolic significance of being the faery realm. Having duly demonstrated his power in this male oriented form of courtship he takes the queen back to the orchard (which traditionally is already a halfway house between human and faery worlds) where he begets a child upon her – Tydorel.

Although there is no specific *geiss* about keeping the relationship secret it goes on for a number of years until discovered accidentally, which spells an end to the relationship for them as well as death for the poor unfortunate who stumbled upon it! Faery law is pretty hard and unforgiving! Unless, as I have suggested elsewhere (in *The Romance of the Faery Melusine*, Skylight Press, 2011) the breaking of the secrecy is akin to a physical law, whereby an artificial set-up is automatically rendered untenable – rather like a pin prick puncturing a balloon.

Something of the possible dangers to the offspring of a human/faery coupling – which is most famously a feature of the Melusine romance where most of her sons have minor or major blemishes – despite his remarkable powers in the human world, to the extent of even becoming a king, Tydorel has the problem that he cannot sleep.

A fact of which he seems unaware until it is unwittingly revealed to him by the son of a widow. (Who has a vague parallel with Perceval, another son of a widow who caused problems by his lack of speech at a crucial moment.) In the case of Tydorel the realisation of his condition brings about a similar catastrophic result – like the denizens of the Graal castle, he immediately disappears back into faeryland!

I WILL TELL YOU A STORY that has just arrived, in a new lai called Tydorel. The king who reigned in Brittany was the last of his line. In his youth he took for wife the daughter of a duke whom married because of her beauty and nobility. He cherished her and surrounded her with honours, and likewise she loved him deeply. Never did he show any jealousy in her regard and she never showed herself unworthy of him. Thus they lived for some ten years but without having any children.

In the course of one summer, as is told by the people of the country, the king stayed at Nantes close by the forest. One day he left for the hunt while the queen went to amuse herself in an orchard for the afternoon, taking her ladies and maidens with her for company. There they played games and several ate the fruit. The queen was dozing under a tree she had chosen, lying on the grass, leaning against a young girl. If the queen felt tired, the young girl felt even more so, and fell asleep too.

When the queen woke, intending to rejoin the others, she could not find anyone and was much astonished. Then looking around she saw a knight advancing slowly through the orchard. He seemed the most handsome man in the world, more than any who presently lived. Magnificent, strong, of fine stature, and richly dressed.

As she saw him come towards her she felt some fear, and began to wonder who he was and got to her feet. Do you know what the lady thought? That it must be some powerful lord come to speak to the king and who, not having found him, had come to see her. Courteously the knight took her by the left hand and thanked her for her gesture of welcome.

"Lady," he said, "I have come here for you, whom I love and desire. Tell me what you desire. I will not press you, but if you feel able to love me with the love that I ask, I will love you loyally in return. If not, I will go away, and leave you. But know then, that you will never know true happiness."

The queen regarded him for a long time, admiring his air and his beauty and was taken with a violent love. She was convinced she could love him, on condition to know who he was, his name and where he came from.

"Oh well," he said, "I will tell you and hide nothing from you. Come with me and you will see, for you cannot otherwise know."

He led her off with him and they left the orchard and went to his horse which was tied to a tree by the reins. The destrier was as white as a flower, and there had never been a more beautiful or better one under the heavens. He took his sword and his arms, mounted the horse, lifted the queen up onto the neck of the horse, and thus they departed.

After a short distance, he put her down near the forest, on a slope, at the foot of a wide hillock at the edge of a lake. Here many had attempted a test – whoever could swim across the lake would see the realisation of all his projects and desires. He made the queen sit on the bank and entered the lake on his horse. The water closed over his head, but he advanced through the deep and so continued for four leagues. The queen did not budge. After coming out on the bank on the far side he returned back to her.

"Lady," he said, "in this forest I come and go as I will. Do not ask me any other questions."

He put her back on the saddle.

"We will love each other for a long time, until they discover us. You will have by me a fine son, whom you will call Tydorel. He will be worthy and brave, and surpass in beauty all knights of this land, and no one will make war on him, for he will have strength over all his neighbours because of his great bravery. He will reign over Brittany but will never be able to close his eyes in sleep. When he comes to the age of reason, have someone watch closely over him. See that he has by him men who turn by turn will sing, keep him happy, and tell him stories he knows, whether interesting or not, for no one would want to take the risk of putting such a man to death."

"Then you will have a beautiful daughter. When the damsel is grown, she will be given in marriage to a count, in this same country. She will have two sons, brave and valiant, hardy and prompt in combat, courteous, courageous, knightly, perfect in every way. Nature will dispense her gifts in them and they will have many children; but because of their origin they will sleep much more than ordinary mortals. From them will be born Count Alain, then his son Conan."

When he had said all this, he returned with her to the orchard, put her down from his horse, fulfilled his desires with her and left.

When he had gone, the maidens who had been far off returned. The queen left with them, saying nothing of her adventure. But she often met with her lover.

When her belly grew the king was happy to know she was pregnant, but did not know the cause. Although some hawked around the neighbourhood a spiteful saying: "Who would want to bring up a child that was not his own?" For this is what had happened to the king; the child was not his own but another's. Yet he was full of joy at the pregnancy of the queen, and most people and his friends knew nothing of the affair.

Her term arrived, and a son came into the world. He was brought up and surrounded by care as he should be, and they baptised him with the name Tydorel. But he was always awake. He could neither drowse nor sleep. All who saw him found this a great wonder. When the child had grown in age and strength, they had to watch with him each night with people on a rota. They told him stories and fables, as his mother had recommended.

His young sister married a count. The faery knight, their father, often came to find the queen, for they loved each other with all their hearts, until a man of the court surprised them.

There had been in the town a bedridden knight, gravely wounded, who had much need of help, being without money. At the cost of great effort he arose and went to ask the queen to grant him some aid in personal funds, for she was naturally generous and gave widely clothes and horses, gold and money to the needy. He found the door of her bed chamber open, entered, and saw the queen lying with her lover.

It caused the couple anxiety and torment on being discovered. The knight, for the last time, held the queen in his arms, then went away never to return. The wounded man felt worse from that moment, his suffering grew and he died next day, at the same hour he had interrupted the lovers.

In course of time the king of Brittany died and the Bretons made Tydorel their lord. They never had a better, nor one who assured such peace in his kingdom. He was courageous, valiant, courteous, generous, liberal, and no one dare go to war against him. He was loved by damsels, an object of admiration for the ladies, his people loved and served him and foreigners feared him.

For ten years he was a powerful king, say the people of the country, and after ten years had passed, went to live in Nantes. He very much loved this country because his mother lived there, and her counsel was there to be found. During the whole time of his stay in the city they set men to take turn to watch by him during the night and tell him stories.

One Saturday, it is said, towards evening, they went to look for the man whose turn had come to sit with the king, and who had not arrived. An apprentice goldsmith, he lived with his old mother, a widow who was feeble and sick, and kept her son by her for a long time at her hearth.

The messengers entered the house and ordered him to go with them to watch during the night in their master's room for he must have some distraction. But the youth refused to leave his mother.

"I do not know any fables or songs," he replied, "nor how to tell a story."

Enraged, the messengers threatened that if he did not go willingly they would take him by force, and lock him up in a place he would not like.

His mother was much afraid of these men. "Dear son," she said, "follow them."

"Leave me alone," he replied. "As I do not know how to sing he will only put me in prison or make me lose an eye."

"Dear son, listen to me, you must go and watch with the king. When he asks you to tell him a story, or narrate a history, or to sing, tell him that you cannot. Then if he becomes angry tell him he was not born of a man. That is why he does not sleep and cannot find rest. This will make him reflect and he will leave you in peace. Go, dear son, in all good faith. And may God make all go well".

Having heard this advice, the son went in all haste to the court and entered the apartments of the king. When night fell, the chamberlains went to bed and the king, seated on a raised bed, spoke to the young man, saying: "Friend, tell me something interesting that will give me pleasure."

"Sire, I do not know how to tell a story and, God help me, I have never sung. It is more than fifteen years since my father died, my mother is a poor woman, has brought me up with many difficulties and I have never left her. I have heard and seen very little, and remembered still less."

"That is unbelievable!" said the king. "There can be no man as ignorant as that. You are a fool, a simpleton! Or you mock me, but when you leave here you will wish you had not!" And he began to threaten him.

"Sire, as I told you, I have seen little, heard little. I have only heard it said by many persons, like a truth, that whoever is not born of a human mortal cannot sleep or find rest."

The king lowered his head in silence, and asked himself why it was he could not sleep. He at last understood what the young man had heard. That he was not born of a simple mortal. He was touched, and overcome by the thought that everyone else in the world could rest, while he stayed wakeful night and day.

He got up, took his sword from its sheath, entered his mother's room, went to her bed and woke her.

On seeing him she cried, "My son, for the love of God, what is this? What do you want here?"

"By God, you will die without mercy at my hands if you do not tell me the truth. Whose son am I? I want to know. The one who watches with me has just said, like a reproach, that whoever cannot sleep cannot be born of a man. Everyone sleeps, yet I stay awake! Why is that, I want to know. I am stupefied by it!"

"I will tell you willingly what I know dear son," she said. "You are my son, I am your mother, but the king was not your father. We lived together ten years without having any children. The king stayed often in this town with his men. One day, he went hunting in the forest and I went to rest in an orchard on the grass and flowers because of the heat. I played with my maidens that I had brought with me, we amused ourselves very much, some amongst them ate the fruit. I was seated under a beautiful bough with a young girl, and I drowsed heavily. The maiden slept as well and when I awoke I could not waken her. Seized with fright, the prey of great fear, I stayed lying there.

"To tell you the whole truth, a knight came towards me, wondrously good looking – Nature had given him all imaginable charms. He was well dressed, tall, of fine figure. He solicited my love with threats and told me that if I did not love him I would never know a happy day; he would go, and I would stay alone, without joy or happiness. I was appalled. He insistently sought my favours; I saw he was so handsome, seductive, courteous, convincing, that I fell in love with him, and he with me.

"He took me out of the orchard, to where he had left his horse, and armed himself with quick and elegant gestures; his equipment was magnificent. Then he mounted his horse, took me by the hand and helped me up to the neck of his mount, and I went off with him. Know that what I tell you is entirely the truth.

"He took me near a wood, at the edge of a great lake where many attempted the test, and made me get down from the horse. He sat me there – and what I tell you is true – left me in haste and rode his horse into the lake, into its deepest part, entirely armed. He went for four leagues, and returned to tell me that he came and went by this way as he pleased. He took no one with him in these comings and goings, and carried all his equipment himself, he did all this alone, without need of company. During the whole time that I was his lover I never saw servant or squire riding with him.

"He returned often and found me and forbade me, on my life, to ask him questions about his nature. I never asked them and respected his orders scrupulously. He would love me, he said, for a long time before we were surprised, but he knew certainly, and repeated it to me, that he would be sought, discovered and recognised. 'But you will have by me,' he added, 'a son who will be brave, handsome, lovable, seductive, courteous, generous, valiant on foot as on horseback. Who would be a noble lord, stay small and not grow very much, but be brave and valorous, and never be overtaken by sleep by night or day. And as you came to the age of reason, each night I must put a rota of men to watch with you and distract you with songs and stories.

"When he had made all these revelations, he took me back to the orchard. Dear son, this is the truth; that day you were conceived. For a long time he returned to see me, for more than twenty years I think, until the day when a knight surprised him, who quickly died because of it. He departed then, never to return, and I do not know where he has gone."

When Tydorel had heard all this he left his mother, returned to his apartments, woke his chamberlains, had his arms brought and mounted his horse. They obeyed his orders and he armed quickly. Spurring away he came to the lake and disappeared into its depths. There he stayed and has never returned.

The Bretons who made this lai believe the story to be true.

·V·
Tyolet

IF THERE WAS A somewhat distant hint of the Graal story in Tydorel, in the gauche son of a widow who could not rise to the occasion of entertaining the half-faery king, we have an almost overt association in Tyolet whose circumstances follow closely the early circumstances of Perceval. He is the son of a widow who lives in a forest and tries to prevent her only son from having any knowledge of knighthood, until in the forest one day he accidentally comes upon a party of knights of King Arthur's court which awakens a desire for knighthood within him.

The difference here is that the knights that Tyolet meets are not human ones. At the conclusion of a hunt he comes upon a faery knight – in red armour, on a white horse with red ears, standing on the other side of a river, transformed from being the stag he has just followed.

There then follows a replication of the amusing dialogue in Chrétien de Troyes' *Conte del Graal* when the young hero questions the knight about all his accoutrements. There is added humour in the lai in his constantly calling the faery knight, and indeed any knight, as a "knight-beast" – as he naively thinks them to be another kind of animal.

After his departure from his mother, who equips him with his late father's armour rather than the country weeds of Perceval, Tyolet makes his way to Arthur's court where he is invited to eat with the king alone at his table. However there is no confrontation with a red knight to gain his armour, although there might be regarded some kind of conflation with the red faery knight. However, from henceforth Tyolet's story departs from that of Perceval. We have instead another sequence that appears in Arthurian romance, of a damsel arriving with a white bratchet hound who seeks a knight to take on the quest of gaining the white foot of an especial stag.

After a number of Arthur's knights have fallen short in this quest Tyolet is given his chance which he executes in the face of many dangers – from crossing a raging river to fighting seven lions that guard the stag. This struggle almost costs him his life. Then in a sequence that has a resonance with part of the Tristan and Iseult cycle Tyolet is betrayed by a knight who tries to claim that *he* is the successful questor.

This is put to rights in part by Gawain, in a role of healer helper that is typical of him in some stories, whilst there is also an important image of Tyolet as wounded knight tended by a faery maiden which also occurs in Chrétien's Graal story and elsewhere. (See R. J. Stewart's *The UnderWorld Initiation* for its importance in ballad lore.)

All comes right in the end and a happy conclusion is hastily contrived, leaving us with the fascinating speculation as to whether much of Tyolet is imperfectly remembered bits of Chrétien's Graal romance, or taps into earlier material independent of Chrétien and his continuators. This is a matter for professional scholars to dispute. From an esoteric point of view the signposts are important whatever the literary provenance.

HIS IS THE LAI of Tyolet. Once, in the time of the reign of King Arthur who governed Britain, which was later called England, and not, I believe, as much peopled as it is today, Arthur enjoyed great renown and had with him his strong proud knights. Many of them were brave and illustrious, but without being of the quality of those who were the most powerful. The best and most generous had the custom of riding by night in search of adventure. They might also ride throughout the day without a squire, and without finding two or three castles, but on dark nights they met fine adventures that they afterwards told at the court when they returned. The learned clerks of that time wrote them down in Latin on their parchments, because there would come a time when all would be pleased to hear them. They tell them now, translated from Latin into French, and the Bretons have made several lais of them, telling about our ancestors.

The one I am going to tell you is about a fine young man, sensible, hardy, proud and brave called Tyolet. He was able to catch beasts by whistling, as many as he wanted. A faery gave him the gift of learning to whistle like this. His mother was a lady who lived in a forest. She lived there night and day, alone, with no house for ten leagues all around.

Her husband, who had been a knight, was dead, and had been so for fifteen years or more. His son Tyolet had grown handsome and big, but had never seen a knight in arms. He lived in the woods with his mother, and held by the love of his mother, had never left the forest. He was courageous and of perfect honesty and went about as he wished, having no other occupation. When the beasts heard him whistle, they ran to him; and he killed what he wanted for food and took them to his mother. He had no sister or brother.

One day his mother asked her son to go into the forest and take a stag. He obeyed her request but went through the forest until nine o'clock in the morning without finding one. Angered with himself for not having met any game, he was about to go back to the house when he saw a great stag under a tree. He whistled. The stag heard and looked at him, but did not wait and went off at a modest pace through the forest. Tyolet followed. The stag went straight to a river which it crossed, but the current was strong, irregular and dangerous.

When the stag had crossed, Tyolet looked behind him and saw a roebuck coming, well fed, big and swift. He stopped and whistled, and when the roebuck approached Tyolet took out his knife and killed it there and then. While he skinned it, the stag that had crossed the river was transfigured and appeared in the guise of a knight. He stood, armed, at the edge of the water, on a horse whose mane floated behind him. The young man stared at him for long time, stupefied. He had never seen anything like it. Marvelling at this strange apparition he could not take his eyes from it.

The knight addressed him in friendly words, asked him who he was, what he was looking for, and what was his name. Without feeling intimidated Tyolet answered he was the son of the widow woman who lived in the forest "and they call me Tyolet for those who want to know my name. Now tell me who you are and what is your name".

The knight, over on the other bank, replied he was called "Knight." Tyolet wanted to know what sort of beast a knight was, where it lived and where it came from.

"In faith" said the knight, "I will tell you truly. It is a redoubtable beast that attacks and eats other beasts. It often lives in the forest but also on the plain."

"My word," said Tyolet, "I never heard such marvels! Since I have known how to walk and started to roam the forests, I have never met a beast of that kind. I know bears, lions and all the other game. There is no beast in the forest that I do not know and can take without fear, but I have never known one like you. You have the air of a hardy beast. Tell me then, knight-beast, what is that on your head? And what is that hung round your neck, that is all shiny and red?"

"Oh I will tell you freely; it is called a helm and is made entirely of steel. And this device before me with a golden band is a shield."

"And what are you dressed in, that coat full of little holes?"

"It is a coat of iron called a hauberk."

"And that which you have as socks? Tell me please."

"They are my iron greaves, of good and beautiful make."

"And tell me what it is that you have at your belt?"

"That is called a sword; it is very beautiful, and has a sharp and solid blade."

"And that long baton you carry? Tell me about that."

"You really want to know?"

"Yes, certainly."

"That is a lance that I carry with me. Now I have answered all your questions."

"I thank you kindly sir. Please God, on whom all count, can I have equipment such as yours, as fine, as becoming, the same coat, the same cloak as you, the same hat? Tell me again, knight-beast, by God and by his feast, if there are other beasts as beautiful as you."

"Yes, surely, I could show you more than a hundred."

A little later, the story tells us, two hundred knights in arms from the king's court came close by. They had carried out his orders, taken a fortress and burnt and reduced it to ashes; they were now returning in three close battalions. Addressing Tyolet, the knight-beast invited him to advance a little and look on the other side of the river. The young man obeyed, and saw the knights in full armour, riding on their destriers.

"My word," he said, "I see there the beasts who have hats on their heads. I have never seen anything like it, nor hats like that. Ah please God and his feast, if only I could be a knight-beast!"

He who stood armed on the bank called out again: "Will you be brave and hardy?"

"Yes I assure you."

"Go then," he said, "and when you see your mother and she says to you 'Dear son, what are you thinking of? What do you want?' tell her you want to resemble the knight-beast you have seen, and that is why you are plunged in thought. She will tell you that she is worried that you have seen this sort of beast that tricks and kills others. Then give her your word that she will see no more of you if you cannot be a beast of this kind and have a helmet on your head. When she hears that, she will bring you all your equipment, hauberk and shield, sword and belt, greaves and long polished lance, as you see here."

Tyolet departed in haste and went back home. He gave his mother the roebuck that he carried and told her the adventure that had happened. His mother was not at all happy and said: "You have just seen a beast that catches and eats the others!"

"Oh well," he said, "so be it. If I cannot be a beast like the one I saw, you will cause me great grief."

In reply to this, she brought him all the arms she possessed and which had belonged to her husband. She armed him as he would have done his son. When she had put him on horseback, he perfectly resembled a knight-beast.

"Do you know, dear son, what you must do? You must go straight to King Arthur but always remember this: take care who you go with, and do not consort with women who give themselves at first sight."

She kissed him and held him close in her arms and he left.

He rode for days by hills and valleys and finally arrived at the royal court.

The valiant and courteous king was sat down for a meal that was richly served. Tyolet entered armed, rode his horse up to the table where King Arthur was seated, but did not say anything to him, not a single word.

"My friend," said the king, "get down from your horse. Come and eat with us and tell me what you want, who you are, and what you are called."

"Ah well, I can tell you that before eating. King, I am called knight-beast, I have cut off the head of many beasts and I am called Tyolet. I know the art of taking game. I am, dear sir, the son of the widow of the forest. She sent me to you in all confidence to teach me good manners. I desire to learn wisdom and courtesy, to know the art of knighthood, joust and tourney, to spend wisely and make gifts, for there has never been nor will be, I believe, a royal court where one could find such a good education, of courtesy, of good lessons, as yours. There you are, I have told you my wishes; now give me your advice."

"Sir knight," said the king, "I will keep you with me, come and eat."

"Sire, great thanks." Tyolet then dismounted, took off his armour, put on a light coat and cloak, washed his hands and went to eat.

But there suddenly arrived a damsel, a proud maiden. I will not speak of her beauty; except to say that neither Dido, in my view, or Helen had so fine a face. She was the daughter of the king of Logres. She sat on a white palfrey, and carried behind her a white bratchet which had a golden bell hanging from its neck, its coat clean and supple. She rode on horseback before the king and saluted him: "King Arthur, may God the Almighty who is in heaven keep you."

"Dear friend, may he protect you too. He who puts the just on His side."

"Sire, I am a young girl, daughter of a king and queen. My father is king of Logres, he and my mother have no other child but me. They ask you, with all the regards due to a king of such prestige, if among your knights there is one hardy and audacious enough to cut off the white foot of a certain stag. Dear sir, my father will give me in marriage to this knight and I will accept him, I would not take any other. No man will have my love, if he does not bring me the white foot of the great and beautiful stag with the shining skin that they say is almost like gold, and is guarded by seven lions."

"My faith," said the king, "I agree to those conditions; whoever brings you the foot of the stag will have you for wife."

"And I too, sir king, I engage to respect them."

They concluded this agreement between them. There was not in the hall any knight, worthy of esteem, who would not accept to go in search of the stag, if only they knew where to find it.

"This bratchet dog," said the young girl, "will lead you to where the stag lives and where it comes and goes."

Before all others, Lodoer had great desire to go, and asked this favour of King Arthur who did not refuse him. Lodoer departed on the quest. He took the bratchet, mounted his horse and went off in search of the stag. The bratchet led him straight to a great wide river, a hideous torrent, 2400 feet wide and almost 100 deep. The bratchet entered the water, according to its instinct, in the belief that Lodoer would follow it, but he did nothing of the kind. He said to himself that he would not enter there, as he did not want to die. And after a moment of reflection, "Who would lose himself for nothing? Whoever keeps misfortune away from his castle keeps a good one."

The bratchet came out of the water and returned to Lodoer who went back to court carrying it on his horse behind him. When he regained the court he gave it back to the young girl who was courteous and beautiful. The king asked him if he brought the foot and Lodoer replied that he left that to others – and became the object of jeers. They mocked him in the hall, but he contented himself by shaking his head: "Then you go," he told them, "to find the foot and bring it back!"

Many tried the test to win the hand of the beautiful girl, but all came back singing the same song as Lodoer, except for one very brave and alert knight, whom they called the knight-beast but whose true name was Tyolet.

He went straight to the king and asked him to keep the maiden there, for he was going on the conquest of the white foot.

"Never" he said, "will I return without the white foot of the stag." The king gave him permission, Tyolet equipped himself, armed head to foot and went to ask the maiden for her white bratchet. She gave it to him and he took his leave.

After a long ride, he and the dog arrived at the ford and the deep and frightening river. The bratchet took to the water and swum straight across. Tyolet went in his turn, mounted on his destrier, and was successful in coming out on firm land. The dog led him to the place where he found the stag. It was guarded by seven lions full of affection for it but Tyolet saw that the seven lions were at pasture in the middle of a meadow. Tyolet advanced and stood a little way off from the stag. Then he began to whistle and the stag docilely approached. At the second whistle of Tyolet the stag stopped still. Tyolet took his sword, seized the right foot of the stag, cut it off at the joint and dropped it into the top of his greaves.

The stag gave a great cry, the lions ran quickly and saw Tyolet. One of them grievously wounded his horse and took away the skin and flesh of its right shoulder. Seeing that, Tyolet struck the lion so violently with his sword that he cut the nerves of its neck, and that lion was out of the game. But his horse fell under him to the ground and Tyolet had to leave it, assailed on all sides. The lions tore his fine hauberk, and the flesh of his arms and sides were so lacerated that it seemed that the lions must devour him. But despite the torn flesh he succeeded in killing them all, only to fall near the beasts who had done him such ill. He had no strength to rise.

But there came a knight mounted on an iron grey destrier. He stopped, looked at the spectacle and kneeled down by Tyolet, who opened his eyes and told him of his adventure. He took the stag's foot from the top of his greaves and gave it to the knight who thanked him for it, very happy with this gift, took his leave and departed.

Then the knight realised that if the knight who had given him the foot remained alive he could perhaps try to reclaim it. He quickly turned about, deciding to kill him to avoid any dispute. He struck Tyolet full in the chest (although he was later cured of this wound) and certain that he had killed him, continued his way to the royal court.

He asked the king to bring forth the maiden to whom he showed the white foot of the stag. But he had not brought back the white bratchet that had led Tyolet to the stag, and which had stayed behind with him. This thought had not occurred to the knight who brought the foot. He said it was he who had killed the stag, and demanded the noble and beautiful damsel for his wife, according to the agreement. But the king, in his wisdom, assembled his court and commanded a delay of eight days to wait for Tyolet, who had not yet returned. The knight could only accept the delay and stayed waiting at the court.

Gawain, the courteous, who knew the conventions well, left in search of Tyolet, taking with him the bratchet which had since returned to court, and which now led him to Tyolet. He found him lying in the field, beside the lions. When he saw the massacre he sorrowed with all his heart. He dismounted and addressed soft words to him, and Tyolet, who could speak only in a weak voice, told him the truth of his adventure.

There then arrived a maiden on a beautiful and dashing mule. She greeted Gawain gracefully. He returned her salute and called her to him, held her close and prayed her with soft and lovable words to take the wounded knight to the healer of the Black Mountain. As Gawain departed she responded to his wishes, taking the knight to leave him with the healer. The healer received him willingly, removed his armour, laid him on a table and washed his wounds that were all full of blood. When they had been well cleaned he saw that he could cure him.

In the meantime Gawain returned to court. Dismounting from his horse in the hall he found the knight who had brought the white foot. The eight days delay decreed by the king were now up. So the knight went to the king and asked him to respect the engagement of which they had spoken and that the king had guaranteed – that the damsel would take for husband whoever had brought back the white foot.

"That is true," said the king.

Gawain, who heard this conversation bounded in straight away.

"It was not like that," he said to the king. "And I ask the liberty before you, to challenge this knight – who is worth no more than a servant, a valet, a squire. I say he is a liar. That he has not taken the foot of the stag in the way he says. What shame for a knight to vaunt himself at the cost of another, to dress in the other's cloak, to shoot with another's arrow, to joust with the hand of the other, to pull out of the bush the deceiving serpent!"

Then addressing the imposter: "No, we will not accept that. What you have said is false. So show your bravery or go elsewhere to seek your fortune. You will not take the maiden."

"Sir Gawain," said the other, "you take me for a villain by saying that I dare not bear my own lance to fight in a duel, that I do not know better than to shoot with another's arrow, or fight with the hand of another and bring the serpent out of the bush. Whoever supports those accusations against me can find me in close field."

While they argued, those in the hall saw the living Tyolet had arrived and dismounted from his horse by the mounting block. The king rose to meet him, threw his arms round his neck, and embraced him affectionately. Tyolet leaned against him who was his lord, Gawain embraced him, then Urien, Kay, Yvain the son of Morgan, Lodoer and all the other knights. Seeing this, the knight who claimed the maiden for bringing the foot that Tyolet had given him, addressed King Arthur again and once more made his claim for her. But Tyolet, hearing this, asked in a quiet and natural tone:

"Sir knight, tell us now before the king, what right you have to the maiden. We would like to know."

"Well I will tell you then; it is because I brought her the white foot of the stag, as she herself and the king have agreed."

"Did you capture the foot of the stag? If it is true, do not deny it."

"Yes," he said, "I took it and brought it here with me."

"And the seven lions. Who killed them?"

The other looked at him without saying a word, but reddened with anger.

"Sir knight," pursued Tyolet, "who was the one who was struck with a sword? And who was the one who struck with it? Tell us, I pray you. For I can avow who was there."

The other, shamed, bowed his head.

"For such infamy," said Tyolet, "you deserve to have your head cut off. I gave you in good faith the foot that I had cut from the stag and you thanked me for it by trying to kill me, or so you intended. Certainly I might have died. I had given you the foot, and I now repent of having done so. You struck me in the body with the sword you wear and hoped to kill me! If you want to justify yourself in the presence of these barons, I tend my gage."

The knight knew he spoke the truth and begged pardon for the stroke. Fearing death more than shame, he did not deny in any way what Tyolet had said. He rendered himself to the king, ready to obey his orders.

On the advice of the king and the barons, Tyolet forgave him. The knight fell to his knees and kissed his foot, and Tyolet raised him up and embraced him affectionately. I have not heard what happened then. The knight gave back the foot, Tyolet took it and gave it to the maiden. She surpassed in beauty the lily or the newly budded rose when it opens in spring. Tyolet asked for her in marriage, King Arthur agreed and the maiden consented. She took him back to her country where he became king and she the queen.

Here ends the lai of Tyolet.

VI

The Hawthorn

AT FIRST SIGHT this seems like a study in forbidden love between brother and sister although in fact there are no blood ties between the young lovers – the son being the offspring of the king and a courtesan, and the daughter the offspring of the queen and a previous husband. So the prohibition is entirely a matter of the personal feelings of the step father and step mother.

But nothing is quite as it first appears in this lai. The damsel chooses to pray for a resolution of their predicament, rather than invoke any faery powers, although the fact that she does so in an orchard has a certain Otherworld ambience to it. The faery element enters almost by accident, insofar that the young man, in seeking to prove his manhood, elects to test his courage by watching at a notorious Ford by a Hawthorn, which by implication brings unspecified terrors. However, as the result of her prayer, the maiden is transported physically, while asleep, to the very Hawthorn Ford.

Here the faeries who appear are three male faeries fully equipped for jousting, and by taking on each one of them in turn the young man proves his prowess, and is even awarded a faery war horse to prove it. And impressed by all these events no barrier is now put in the way of the two lovers getting married.

As in most faery stories a form of prohibition or *geiss* is connected with the horse. Despite a warning that if it is taken off the bridle he will lose it, in later years his wife does this very thing – apparently to see what would happen – and consequently loses it.

Altogether it seems a hotchpotch of faery traditions that have been linked together almost in a random way. However, the traditional faery dynamics of Hawthorn and Ford between the worlds are plainly represented here as a test of valour, and apparently with the sanction of Heaven insofar that it is by prayer that the damsel is transported to the faery testing ground.

T FIRST SIGHT lais may seem to be lies – but do not take them to be mere dreams. I vouch for the truth of these adventures of times past and have told them in many places. I use stories that have been preserved at Caerleon, in the church of St. Aaron, and are known in Brittany and many other countries. Now, as the remembrance has been preserved, I will tell you an adventure of two children that has always been obscure.

There was in Brittany a young man of great beauty, brave and courteous, son of the king, but born of a concubine. His father and his step-mother were of higher extraction than he. The king cherished him, having no other child, and the queen also loved him with a deep affection.

On the other hand, the queen had had a daughter by a former husband, a wise and courteous maiden, a young damsel with a delicate complexion. The two children were not yet very old. The boy, the eldest, was only seven. Both, each as beautiful as the other, willingly played together in perfect accord. They loved each other so much that each was upset if the other was not at their side.

It was thus they were raised together. Together they came and went, played at their games, and those who looked after them allowed them every freedom, not separating them for meals, but with only one exception – forbidding them to sleep together.

But when they came of an age that Nature permitted, they began to awaken to love, and after these infantile attachments, Nature lodged in them a totally other kind of love. Each felt attraction for the other and they had only one desire, to embrace and lie together. Nature ordered things so well that their new love united them, and their feelings took a deeper course. The more each one became conscious of the other the greater grew their love. Their love was sincere, and had they given as much care to hiding their love for each other, they would have easily avoided disgrace. But they were soon discovered.

One day, the fine and valiant young man returned from hunting water fowl and had a headache because of the heat. He went to lie down alone in a room apart to escape the noise and relieve his malaise a little. His friend was in the queen's apartments at her lessons. But when she learned of his return, without waiting and without a word to anyone she ran to the room where he was laid on the bed. He received her with joy, for he had not seen her all day, and without the least hesitation she lay down beside him and kissed him tenderly a hundred times.

They prolonged these moments of folly too long, for the queen saw them; she followed her daughter to the room quietly, found the door open, and no lock preventing her, entered and found them intertwined upon the bed, with all evidence of the love they felt for each other.

Deeply disturbed, she grasped the young girl, covered her with reproaches, inspired in her a great fear, and imposed a heavy punishment. The young girl broke down, the young man in consternation heard the blows, the reprimands and the punishment that her mother inflicted on her daughter. He did not know what to do or say, but knew their secret had been discovered and that his lover was lost to him. Concerned for her and ashamed for what they had done, he dare not leave his room and abandoned himself to his grief: "Alas," he said, "How can I live without her? God! What ill fortune and what fault! Fool that I am to be so mistrusted! If I can not recover my lover, I would rather lose my life."

While he lamented thus, the queen went to find the king and insisted with all her authority that they guard the young girl and that the young man cease to be near her. The king promised to watch over his son at court, and thus the young people were separated. "And see," she added, "that no-one knows anything of this."

As a result of this conversation the young man, full of sadness, went to find his father and addressed him respectfully: "Sir, I seek a favour of you. If you want to help me, make me a knight, and I will go to another country to acquire renown. I have seen enough of the ways of my house and I am not yet good at handling a sword."

The king agreed to his request, but proposed he stay a year at court and during that time follow the tourneys, and keep the passage at the defiles. The young man accepted the offer and continued to live with his father, and the young girl with her mother. But both were so closely watched there was no chance of seeing each other, or communicating by messenger or servant. Yet love tortured them still.

Eight days before St John, the same year that the young man was made knight, the king returned from the hunt with an abundant bag of birds and game. That evening, after supper, he sat at table to amuse himself along with many knights of the court, his son with him. They listened to the lai of Aélis that an Irishman sang sweetly accompanied by his rote. After this lai, he began another in perfect silence and great attention. It was the lai of Orpheus. And when he had finished the knights took up their conversations again and told of adventures that had happened to them or that they had seen in Brittany.

There was among them a young girl who spoke of the Ford of the Hawthorn on St John's night, when things happened more than any other night of the year, and no cowardly knight dare take up the test.

The young man, who did not lack courage, listened attentively. He had never gone on adventure since he had been given his sword and this seemed worth a strike for fame so as not to be thought a coward. At the end of the young girl's story, he appealed to the king and all the barons, great and small, to pay heed to him.

"Lords," he said, "I want to go there during the night of which the young girl speaks, to take the adventure of the Ford of the Hawthorn, however hard it may be."

The king was saddened on hearing this and tried to hold the project to be childish. "Dear son, " he said, "forget such folly."

But he replied that he would not, and wanted to go anyway. Seeing that his son would not be put off it, the king no longer opposed it. "Very well," he said, "by the grace of God go! Be brave and confident. And may God give you good luck!"

Everyone went to bed and the young knight waited impatiently until the seventh day. His lover almost died with fear when she heard he was going to this test of watching all night at the perilous Ford. But when the night came he was full of good hope. In arms, he mounted a good horse and rode to the Ford of the Hawthorn.

What did the damsel do? She went alone to an orchard to pray God to keep her friend safe and sound. Sat under a tree, she sighed and lamented, and sorrowed to the depths of her heart: "Holy father," she prayed, "if it is possible that a prayer brings comfort, have pity Lord, help my love and me come together! No one knows the hard life I lead. And no one could imagine it, except one who loves another from whom he is for ever deprived. Such a one, yes, would feel it in his heart." Thus prayed the maiden, seated on the grass.

They looked for her a long time, without being able to find her. No one knew where she was as she abandoned herself to her despair of love, in tears and lamentations. The day declined and night fell, and overtaken with grief, she lay down under the tree and slept. Hardly had she fallen asleep, I do not know how, or who could have taken her from under the tree to put her down at the Ford of the Hawthorn as her lover was approaching.

He was not slow to appear and found her there sleeping. Suddenly awakened, not knowing where she was, fearful and amazed, she hid her face, but her lover reassured her. "Come," he said, "do not be afraid, since I want to marry you. If you are able to talk, tell me what has happened, how you come to be here so mysteriously."

The young girl was reassured, but when she saw she was not in the orchard asked the knight: "Where am I then?"

"Damsel, at the Ford of the Hawthorn, where many adventures come, some good, some bad."

"Oh my God! May we be out of danger! God has heard my prayer."

This was the first adventure that this night brought to the knight. His lover ran to embrace him; he put foot to ground and took her tenderly in his arms, gave her a hundred kisses, and sitting under the Hawthorn, she told him how she had gone to the orchard, prayed they be united, and fallen asleep.

Having heard this tale, as he looked across to the other side of the Ford he saw a knight had arrived, lance couched to attack. His armour was red, as were the ears of his horse, the rest of its body entirely white. He did not cross the Ford but stayed where he was. The young man told his lover the time had come for him to prove his prowess, but she must not budge from where she was. He leaped back on his horse, happy to have the occasion to joust, and crossed the Ford, resolved to put all his strength into the encounter.

With all the force of their horses they exchanged violent blows on their shields and the wood flew as their lances clashed. Without grave wounds, both fell to the ground then hastened to remount. Once more in the saddle, they held their shields before their chests and lowered their ash wood lances. The young man, shamed to have fallen under the eyes of his love at the first joust, struck so forcefully that under his blows the red knight was unseated and voided the saddle. Having unhorsed his adversary under the eyes of the damsel, the young knight seized the other's destrier by the reins, and came back across the Ford, leaving the vanquished stretched out on the other side.

But the other did not stay long on the ground, as he soon received help. Two other knights came forward, put him on the saddle of another horse, and when he had left the two of them crossed the ford. Once on dry land, they did not say a word but made signs that they wanted to joust. The young man was concerned at this, for they were not on equal terms. But he had no reason to be frightened, for each of them fought singly as a true knight, without the aid of the other.

One stood aside peacefully, while the other adjusted his arms, and with courtesy waited for the young man to engage him. When the latter saw this he was quickly reassured and recalled he had come to the Ford with the intention of fighting to gain glory and honour.

Each charged the other and their lances broke noisily, without either voiding the saddle. But their horses were reversed, so each put foot to ground and fought on with their swords. With the combat so hotly engaged, one of them would soon have been wounded, but the other knight came forward and parted them to put an end to the fight.

Then he courteously addressed the young man: "Friend," he said, "now joust with me, then we will go. We have no desire to stay until the rise of dawn. If you were put to evil or killed by mischance, it would add nothing to your renown. They would speak no more of you, and no one would know of your adventure for it would remain unknown for ever. Your damsel holds the good destrier of Castile that you have conquered by your prowess. You will never have such a marvellous one, as long as you keep him on the bridle. There will be no need to give him food and you will never find one more rapid. But if you take off his bridle you will lose him. Now, be not disappointed, you have proved most valiant and hardy."

The young man heard these reasonable words, and the prediction, but wanted to joust again to prove himself more worthy. He took up arms and reins, seized an ash wood lance, and took his distance from the knight. They came together and struck so hard that their shields were split and broken, but they did not lose their stirrups and stayed firm. Then the young man hit his opponent such a blow that would have knocked him to the ground if he had not gripped the neck of his horse. The young man continued through, drew his sword and turned, but the knight was ready for him, eager to start again. Each struck great blows with their swords but each stayed in the saddle.

The young girl was seized with fear at the sight, and in agonies for her friend. She implored the knight who had fought the first joust to separate them, and he was courteous and did so with good will. Then with his companion he crossed the Ford and they disappeared.

The young man did not delay but went quickly to his lover, still trembling under the Hawthorn, and put her on his horse before him. The test was over.

At day break they arrived back at court. Seeing him, the king was filled with joy, and also amazement. He welcomed the young girl as the great lord he was, the queen at his side. That day the king convoked his court, his barons and all his men, to rule in justice a quarrel between two barons who were reconciled before him.

In the presence of this assembly all were told the whole adventure. Of what had happened when the young knight went to mount guard at the Ford, his meeting with the young girl under the Hawthorn, the jousts and the conquest of the destrier taken from his adversary. The knight went everywhere with this horse, that was useful to him on many occasions, and lavished on him careful attention. He took the young girl as his wife, and kept the destrier until one day, when she wanted to know the truth about the horse so dear to her husband, she took off the bridle and thus it was lost.

The Bretons made a lai of the adventure I have told you. As it took place at the Ford, they did not want to give it any other name than the Lai of the Hawthorn. It started and finished well, but they did not tell me the name of the two children.

VII

Mélion

MÉLION IS A YOUNG MAN who has very high standards when it comes to seeking a wife or lover. So much so that the whole of female society turns against him, which causes him to fall into depression. However by way of consolation the king grants him a very special fief in the country, by the sea, which seems to be ideal in every way. It is here, whilst riding in the forest he comes upon a most beautiful damsel, and in traditional fashion the two of them are married. She does have certain faery qualities, although does not appear to be a faery, despite being clad in red, the faery colour. She claims that she is the daughter of the King of Ireland – which may possibly be a coded reference to Faeryland – and has always loved him from afar.

The two are married and she bears him two children, although nothing more is mentioned of them. However, when out hunting with his wife – a somewhat unusual circumstance – they come upon a great stag which his wife insists he must hunt, for if she does not eat its flesh she will starve herself to death.

This is somewhat of a tall order but Mélion is able to fall back to the recourse of a magic ring, which is capable of turning him into a wolf. Feeling that he is more likely to hunt the stag down in this guise, he asks his wife to touch him with the ring and the metamorphosis takes place. He rushes off in pursuit of the stag only to find that in his absence his wife has deserted him and apparently returned to Ireland – or Faeryland.

No reason is given for any of this, but one might well assume that the magic ring was originally given to him by his faery wife who had just this kind of thing in mind and, having presumably tired of the human life, decided to despatch him in this way and go back to her own people. The polar colours of the two stones in the ring are also of interest, as both are faery colours, and one of the distinctions between human and faery blood is said to be that one is red and the other white (cf. Wendy Berg, *Red Tree, White Tree*, Skylight Press, 2010). The rest of the lai concerns the adventures of the man/wolf or werewolf and how he eventually manages to return to human form through the intervention of King Arthur.

If there is a moral in this story it might well be that it is better to lower one's standards and marry a human wife, rather than opt for the ideal beauty but somewhat treacherous potential of a faery (or Irish?) one. Although maybe Mélion asked for trouble in the first place by his lowly opinion of women.

N THE DAYS when King Arthur reigned, conquering kingdoms, which produced rich gifts for his knights and barons, he had with him a young man by the name of Mélion. He was brave and courteous and loved by all, had great courage and was agreeable company. The king had a brilliant court, prized throughout the whole world for its courtesy and prowess, and whenever they made a vow they respected it scrupulously.

However, Mélion made one that caused him great misfortune. He vowed he would never love a maiden, no matter how noble or beautiful she might be, who had loved or even mentioned the name of another man. Time passed. And many heard of his vow, reported in various places, and damsels who learned of it conceived a great hatred for Mélion. Those who were in the service of the queen (there were more than a hundred) agreed in saying they would never love Mélion or ever address him with a single word. Not a lady wanted to look at him nor any young girl speak to him.

When Mélion learned of this he was deeply affected, and he lost his desire to seek adventure or to carry arms and so his renown suffered from it. The king knew this, and was moved by it and called him to him.

"Mélion," he said, "what has become of your wisdom, your renown, your bravery? Hide nothing from me – tell me why you are so downcast. If you want some land or a castle or whatever else I possess in my kingdom, you can have it, whatever it is. I would be happy to give you joy if I could. I have a castle by the sea, which has no equal in the world, it is magnificent, surrounded by woods, rivers and the forests that you like so much. I will give it to you to put you into a good humour."

Thus the king gave him the fief. Mélion thanked him and went off to his castle taking with him a hundred knights. The country pleased him, and also its forest, which he liked very much. After a year there, he became attached to the country, and found in the forest all the pleasures he wished.

One day he went hunting with his foresters and huntsmen, who had great affection for their liege lord, who was a mirror of honour, and they came upon a great stag but lost it.

Mélion stopped in the woods to listen for its track, accompanied by a squire who had two greyhounds on a leash. In a green and beautiful place Mélion came upon a young girl on a beautiful palfrey in rich attire. She was dressed in vermilion silk, prettily stitched with lace, under an ermine mantle, and no queen could have worn anything more beautiful. Her shoulders, her body were ravishing, her hair fair, her mouth well designed, the colour of a rose, she had lively eyes, clear and laughing, and was beautiful in every way. She was alone, without company, slim and becoming.

Mélion saluted her graciously: "Fair one," he said, "I salute you in the name of the glorious king Jesus. Tell me where you were born and who brought you here."

"I will tell you," she replied, "without a lie. I am of high birth and a noble line. I have come from Ireland to tell you I have never loved anyone but you and would never love another. I have often heard elegies about you, and have wanted to love you alone and never would I have another love."

When Mélion heard that, his wishes were fulfilled. He held her close to him and kissed her more than thirty times. Then he called all his men and told them of the adventure. At the sight of the maiden, they thought they had never seen one as beautiful in the whole kingdom. Mélion took her to his castle amid great joy and married her in a magnificent ceremony. He was full of happiness. The celebrations lasted 15 days. For three years he cherished her and had two sons by her, which again added to his happiness.

One day he went into the forest, taking with him his dear wife. As they entered a wooded grove, casting his eyes on a thicket Mélion saw a great stag standing there.

He called his wife, laughing. "Lady," he said, "I will show you an enormous stag. Look there, in the thicket."

"Well Mélion," she said, "if I cannot eat the flesh of that stag, I will never eat another thing." And as the stag fled, head down, she fell senseless from her palfrey.

Mélion lifted her up, but was unable to comfort her as she began to cry bitterly.

"Lady," he said, "do not weep, I pray you. I have a ring here on my finger. It has in its setting two stones without equal; one is white, the other red. They both have marvellous virtues. Touch my head with the white when, with my clothes removed, I am quite naked, and I will become a great wolf with powerful body. For the love of you I will then catch the stag and bring you its flesh. Wait for me here and keep my clothes I pray you. I leave you mistress of my life and death, for if I am not touched with the other stone all will be lost, I will never become a man again."

Mélion took off his clothes, assisted by a squire, and lay naked enveloped only in his cloak. His wife touched him with the ring and he became a great strong wolf.

The wolf ran towards the place where the stag had been standing and followed its trail, but would need to be strong to catch it and take it.

"Let him hunt as he wishes," said the lady to the squire. She mounted her horse without waiting, led the squire with her, and returned directly to Ireland, her country. She arrived at a port, found a boat, and spoke with the mariners who helped her sail to Dublin, a city on the sea which belonged to her father, the king of Ireland. She was welcomed with joy, and from then on, had nothing to desire. But let us return to Mélion.

In the stag hunt he pressed and pursued it and soon brought it down. He took a great piece of meat that he carried in his jaws and returned in haste to where he had left his wife. But he could not find her; she had gone back to Ireland!

Anxious at her absence, he did not know what to do. Complete wolf though he was, he had kept the mind and spirit of a man. He waited until evening, and saw a boat that was about to load and go that night by sea to Ireland. He went to one side, waited until night fell and crept on it at great risk, not caring more for his life. He hid himself and crouched beneath an awning. The mariners left, and profiting from favourable winds raised the sails, and guided by the stars, passed the cape to Ireland as all wished.

Next day at day break they were in view of the coast of Ireland. When they approached the port, Mélion came out from his hiding place, and jumped out of the boat onto the bank. The mariners cried aloud and ran after him, beat at him with their oars and one of them with a club and very nearly caught him. Happy to have escaped he climbed a hill that looked out over the country where he knew his enemies lay. He still had a piece of meat that he had brought from his country, and ate it, tortured with hunger and weak from the crossing.

He entered a forest and found bullocks and cows and opened his hostilities. He killed more than a hundred, for a start. The men who were in the woods saw the massacre of the beasts and ran to the town. They told the king there was a great wolf in the forest that ravaged the country and had greatly damaged their herds, but the king gave little importance to what they said.

Mélion went by forests, mountains and moorland and made ten wolves his companions. He flattered and caressed them so they attached themselves to him and would all do his will. They ran across the country, away from the main highways, putting men and women to grief. For a whole year they devastated the country, ruining the region. As they were always on their guard the king never managed to trap them.

One night they had travelled far, and harassed, were overcome with fatigue. They entered a wood to rest, near Dublin, on a height close to the sea overlooking a plain. All around them extended a vast country. It was there they were surprised and trapped. A peasant saw them and ran to the king.

"Sire," he said, "the eleven wolves are lying in the Round Wood."

At these words the king happily called his men.

"Sirs," he said to them, "listen to me well. This man has seen the eleven wolves in my forest."

They put all round the woods the traps they usually used to take boars. This done, the king mounted his horse and invited his daughter to go with him to see the hunt. They arrived discreetly at the wood, without making any noise, and surrounded it with a crowd of men carrying axes and clubs, and some with drawn swords. They had a thousand dogs that they excited and which did not take long to find the wolves.

Mélion saw they were discovered and realised he was in danger. The dogs closed in on the wolves which fled toward the traps. They were all killed and cut to pieces, none of them escaped alive – except Mélion who was successful in leaping over the traps. Saved thanks to his cleverness he hid in a great forest. The men returned to the city and the king was fully satisfied, happy to have taken ten wolves out of eleven, only a single one left was a good end to the affair.

"It was the biggest," said his daughter, "he could still do us harm."

When he had escaped, Mélion climbed a mountain, greatly afflicted and sad to have lost his wolves.

For a long time he led a hard existence, but would soon have help. King Arthur was coming to Ireland to re-establish peace in the country; discords reigned there and he desired to reconcile the adversaries and enrol them in his war of conquest against the Romans.

The king came without ceremony, with no great following, only twenty knights. The weather was fine, the boat luxurious and imposing, well equipped, with good pilots, well provided with men and arms. The shields were suspended outside and Mélion recognised them; at first the shield of Gawain, then he distinguished that of Yvain and of King Yder, from which he derived great joy. He also recognised the shield of the king and was delighted, for he thought to awaken his pity.

They took sail towards dry land, but because of a contrary wind could not enter the port. Discouraged, they drove towards another port two leagues from the city. There had once been a great castle there, but now a ruin. When they landed, evening had fallen and it was night.

The king entered the port, exhausted by the crossing and called his seneschal to find them somewhere to sleep for the night, who with his chamberlains left the boat and went to the castle. They took candles with them and lit them, and with covers and carpets all was made ready. Then the king disembarked and entered his lodging, happy to find it so fine.

Losing no time, Mélion went straight to the boat berthed near the castle and recognised it perfectly. He was sure that without the help of the king, he would die in Ireland, but did not know how to approach him, wolf as he was, and deprived of language.

All the same he went and took his chance. He entered the hall at risk of death and ran straight towards the king. He fell at his feet and did not dream of getting up again. There was general stupefaction.

"Here is a marvel," said the king, "this wolf has come to me! See, he is tame, do not touch him, do not lay a hand on him."

When the meal was ready and the barons had washed their hands, the king washed his in turn and sat. They put before them the tablecloths, and the king called Yder and had him sit by his side. At the feet of the king lay Mélion who easily recognised all the barons. The king looked at him many times, and gave him some bread which Mélion ate. Seized with astonishment, the king said to Yder: "Look, for sure, this wolf is tame."

He gave it another piece of bread and the wolf ate it hungrily.

"Sire," said Gawain, "this wolf does not behave like a beast."

The barons talked between themselves and agreed they had never seen a wolf so courteous. The king had a basin of wine put before the wolf. On seeing it the wolf drank with great relish, that the king remarked with interest.

After rising from table and washing their hands, the barons went out to the shore. The wolf attached itself to the steps of the king wherever he went, and nothing happened to stop him. When the king decided to go to bed, for he was very tired, the wolf still followed him. He could not be separated from the king and lay down at his feet.

The King of Ireland learned from messengers that Arthur had come to see him, and was very pleased and joyful. He rose in the morning at dawn and went to the port with his barons. They welcomed each other heartily. Arthur showed him great affection, full of regard, and the other, seeing him come to him, did not want to be distant, and rose and embraced him. Their horses were close by, and they mounted their saddles to go to the city.

On his palfrey the king took care of his wolf, careful not to abandon him, and the beast did not quit his stirrup. The king of Ireland was pleased with the coming of Arthur, it was a magnificent and imposing procession. Arriving in Dublin, they put foot to ground before the great palace. When Arthur entered, the wolf held him by the tail of his clothing. When the king sat, the wolf lay at his feet.

They had a sumptuous and copious feast in the palace and were served with abundance. Looking across the hall, Mélion saw the one who had taken his wife, certain that he had passed the sea to go to Ireland. He leaped and seized him by the shoulder and the baron could put up no resistance. The wolf threw him down in the middle of the hall and would have killed him had not the servants of the king run in with batons and stakes. They would have straight away put the wolf to death had not King Arthur cried: "Do not touch him I order you! That wolf is mine!"

"Lords," said Yder, the son of Urien, "you act badly. If the wolf had not reason to hate this man he would not have attacked him."

"Yder," said Arthur, "you are right."

"You must tell," he said to the man, "why he attacked you or we will leave him to kill you."

The man gave a great cry, implored the king's pity and told him the whole truth. How the lady came to Ireland having touched her husband with the ring, and swore to all that had happened.

"I am sure," said Arthur, addressing the king of Ireland, "that that is the truth. I am reassured at the disappearance of my vassal. Bring me the ring, and your daughter who wore it, who has cruelly tricked her husband."

The king went quickly to his room with Yder. He so cajoled his daughter that she gave him the ring and he took it to King Arthur.

At the sight of the ring Mélion recognised it immediately, he went and knelt at the feet of the king and licked them. Arthur wanted to touch him with the ring there and then but Gawain objected: "Dear uncle," he said, "do not do that! Take him into a private room so he is not shamed before the people."

The king took Gawain and Yder and the wolf to his room. Once there, he shut the door and put the ring to the head of the wolf. First there appeared the face of a man, and then all his appearance changed as he took on human form again and recovered the use of speech.

Mélion fell at the feet of the king, and they covered him with a cloak. When they saw he was transformed into a man, all showed great joy. The king had tears in his eyes and asked him how this had been, by what fault they had lost him. He sent his chamberlain to bring rich clothes with which he clad and adorned him. All the house marvelled at seeing Mélion return.

The king of Ireland brought his daughter and presented her to Arthur to dispose of as he wished, to be condemned to the stake or otherwise put to death.

"I will touch her with the stone," said Mélion, "it will not be otherwise."

"No," said Arthur, "you will not do that, because of your fine children."

At the supplication of all the barons Mélion let himself yield. King Arthur stayed in Ireland the necessary time to secure an agreement. Then he returned to his kingdom taking Mélion with him, who was very happy to have left his wife in Ireland, and wished her to all the devils. Never could he love her for treating him in the way you have heard. He refused to take her back, let her burn or be hanged, it was all one to him!

"Who believes in his wife blindly," he said, "will be a certain victim. You cannot believe all a woman says."

That is the true lai of Mélion, affirmed by the barons, that ends here.

VIII

Doon

T HERE IS NO clear indication of who might be the faery in this lai – the proud maiden and heiress of the kingdom of Scotland, who lives in a House of Maidens, and places an impossible task upon any who seek to be her husband (plainly to journey on horseback from Southampton to Edinburgh in one day is beyond all normal human or animal possibility) or Doon, a Breton knight, who has a horse by the name of Bayard, which is apparently well up to the task.

This is not the only test, for others who have preceded him, and have claimed to have done the journey in the required time, have come to grief when put to rest in a bed so softly furnished that they die in their sleep. At least this is the only known cause of their death. Doon, however, is up to this trick, or trap, and by staying awake all night before a burning fire survives the night. Even so the proud damsel demands a third test, which is for his horse to gallop in a single day as fast as a swan can fly. This last test achieved, there is nothing to prevent Doon from marrying the proud heiress of Edinburgh.

However, having conceived a child upon her, Doon promptly leaves his wife and returns to Brittany, but leaves a ring which she is to give to their son when he is born, with instructions that when he is grown, to send him to France to be made and prove himself a knight. The now grieving mother performs all this over the following years until at a tournament at Mont St Michel the father and son joust. The son wins the field, and then, by the fact of wearing the ring, is recognised and restored to his father – a favourite folklore motif – after which Doon returns with his son to Edinburgh and his deserted and chastened bride.

It is difficult to tell which of the protagonists might be of the faery kind. Certainly the heiress with her triple tests, one of them impossible, the second potentially lethal (and quite mysterious in its operation), and the third, also apparently impossible, seems to have a faint faery resonance. But on the other hand Doon, with his obviously magical horse and dispensing a ring (although not apparently a magical one) and his knowledge of the future sex of his child, if nothing else, has greater faery characteristics. Among which may be a lesson to a somewhat too proud and picky human bride.

MANY PEOPLE KNOW the lai of Doon, every good harpist knows how to play the melody but I want to tell you the story to which the Bretons have given the name the Lai of Doon.

If I am not mistaken, near to Edinburgh, a town in the north, lived a young girl marvellously beautiful and courteous. She was heiress of the kingdom, as there was not another lord, and she lived in Edinburgh because the place pleased her so much, by reason of which she and her damsels called it the House of Maidens.

She of whom I speak was proud of her riches and disdained all young men in the country. There was not one of so illustrious renown that she wanted to love or to take for husband or to be betrothed to, and she said she refused to live in servitude under the pretext of marriage.

All the important people of the country went and prayed to her, they wished to see her married, but she gave them all a formal refusal. She would only take for husband, she said, one who for love of her would accept to make in a single day the journey from Southampton-on-Sea to her residence. That one, she said, she would take for a husband, thinking thus to get rid of the importunate. So they left her in peace.

But things did not remain like that. When the men of the country learned this – and I tell you truly – many attempted the test following the imposed itinerary, mounting great and strong horses to assure a rapid journey. Most could not accomplish the journey in a day.

Any who claimed they had done so, when they arrived at the castle, were met by the damsel and received with honour, but then taken alone to her apartments to rest, where they perished traitorously. She had the beds prepared with good sheets and covers, and these unfortunate ones, completely broken with fatigue, died in their sleep in their soft beds. When the chamberlains found them dead and carried the news to their lady she was very satisfied to hear it.

The tale of the proud damsel spread far. In Brittany, over the sea, a hardy and valiant knight, wise, courteous and enterprising, heard tell of it; he was called Doon.

He possessed a good horse by the name of Bayard, very fast, that he would not have exchanged for two castles. Confident of his destrier he decided to take up the challenge, to see if he could make the conquest of the maiden and her kingdom.

As soon as possible he crossed the sea and arrived at Southampton. He sent the damsel his messenger and informed her of his arrival, praying her to send some of her men of confidence to attest that he had truly left on the day fixed for his departure. When she had heard the messenger she sent some of her men to confirm the day that Doon would leave for her country.

One Saturday morning Doon set off. He rode so well that by the same evening he had accomplished the trip. Arriving at Edinburgh, he was received with joy by the knights and servants. There was not one, great or small, who did not honour him, or put themselves at his service and make him welcome. After meeting with the damsel, they led him to a room to rest, where he demanded they bring him some very dry logs before he lay down to rest.

They met with his wishes and he closed the door firmly, not wanting to be observed. With a tinder box he made a fire, and approached the flames to warm himself. Throughout the night he did not lie in the bed that they had prepared for him. If, overtaken with fatigue, he had profited from this good bed, misfortune would not have been long in coming. The more one lies on hardness, the less one feels lassitude and more quickly recovers one's strength.

In the morning, when it was day, he opened the door, lay down on the bed, covered himself comfortably and went to sleep. The guardians of the room who thought to find him dead found him in perfect health and rejoiced. He rose at the first hour, washed and dressed and went to find the damsel to hold her to her promise.

"Friend," she replied, "it cannot be so yet. It is necessary to put a further test to your horse. In a single day it must go as quickly as a swan can fly. Then I will freely take you as my husband."

He asked for a delay, the time for Bayard to rest and regain his breath. The departure was fixed for the fourth day. Doon set off *en route*, Bayard galloped, the swan flew and, marvel of marvels, without exerting itself the horse ran quicker than the swan could fly.

That night they arrived at a magnificent castle where Doon found good lodging and his horse a good stable. He stayed there as long as he pleased and, when he desired, returned to Edinburgh and required that they honour the promise made. The beauty could no longer play with him. She summoned her barons, and on their advice took Doon for her husband, that made him lord of the realm.

When they were married, Doon spent three days at a solemn plenary court. The fourth day he rose early, called for his horse, recommended his wife to God, and told her he was returning to his own country. The lady was in tears, now sorry at his departure. She implored him tenderly, but in vain. She begged him to stay, saying that she was betrayed.

He did not want to hear any of that, impatient to leave.

"Lady," he said, "I am going away, and don't know if I will ever see you again. You are pregnant by me, and will have a son I think. Give him my gold ring when he is grown and tell him to keep it. It will allow him to find me. Then send him to the king of France who will see him raised and educated."

He gave her the ring and he went off without further delay. Saddened, she complained bitterly; she was indeed pregnant. At the birth of her son she showed great joy. She kept him close to her, and surrounded with affection until he was of an age to mount a horse and go hunting in the forest or after water fowl. She gave him his father's ring advising him to look after it well.

In due time the young man was sent to the King of France, taking much gold and silver. Generous with his gifts, he made himself much loved at that court, where he had a perfect education.

He stayed for a long time in France and when the king made him a knight he frequented tourneys across the country, renowned for his valour far and near. There was not in the kingdom any so valiant as he. Whenever he heard tell of some need, he was the first to go to help. He attracted the admiration of knights and acquired a fine reputation, always surrounded by numerous companions.

One day he went to take part in a tourney at Mont St Michel in Brittany, desiring to make the acquaintance of the Bretons. No one engaged so much in the jousts or had such success. His father saw him from the opposing camp, and was impatient to measure himself against this young man. Lance couched, he ranged up to measure up the bravery of this adversary.

They charged one against the other, exchanged formidable blows, and the son beat his father! If he had known it was his father he would have profoundly regretted it, but he did not know, and nor did Doon know it was his son who grievously wounded him in the arm. At the end of the tourney, he came to talk to the young man, and asked him: "Who are you, friend, you who beat me on horseback?"

"Sir," replied the young man, "I don't know how that happened! Those who were there will know perhaps."

At these words, Doon said "Show me your hands."

The young man took off his gloves and extended his two hands.

On seeing them Doon recognised the ring he had given his wife, and his heart was filled with joy and exhilaration. By this ring he recognised his son.

"Young man," said he before everyone, "when you jousted with me just now, I thought you must be of my lineage, there was about you a great bravery. Never has any knight given me blow to make me fall from my horse, and no one has struck so hard as to beat me. Come and embrace me, I am your father. Your mother is full of pride, I obtained her hand at the cost of great efforts. After having married her, I left, as I no longer wanted to see her, but I left her this ring and told her to give it to you when she sent you to France."

"Sir," said his son, "that is the truth!"

They joyfully embraced and went off together to share the same lodgings. Then they returned to Scotland.* The son took his father to his mother's house, who still loved her husband and ardently desired his return. She welcomed him back and they lived surrounded by honours.

Of the story of Doon, and of his good horse and the son he cherished, and the voyage he undertook for love of his lady, the Bretons made the music for this lai and called it Doon.

---

* Actually the lai says that they returned to England, but to a Breton jongleur there was no great sense of insular geography – as may be seen from ideas of the distance from "Southampton-on-Sea" to Edinburgh!

·IX·

The Trot

T IS ARGUABLE if this lai is really a faery one, but it entails a vision of couples emerging from a forest, and there is a certain resonance between faery tradition and the cult of Courtly Love that became fashionable in 12th century courtly circles in western Europe. The faery element in this short but famous lai is a vision of how it is important to obey the laws of love, and the vision that appears to the Lord of Morois follows closely a scenario first described by André le Chaplain in his famous rule book *The Art of Courtly Love* that was published towards the end of the 12th century. The lai is also mentioned in passing by André Lebey in *Le Roman de la Mélusine,* translated by me as *The Romance of the Faery Melusine* (Skylight Press, 2011.)

WANT TO TELL YOU an adventure that has been put into rhyme from start to finish. What I am going to tell you actually happened, without the word of a lie.

It was a strange adventure that once happened in Brittany to a powerful knight, hardy, courageous, full of audacity. He was a knight of the Round Table of King Arthur who knew perfectly to honour a good knight and was prodigious with rich gifts. This knight was called Lorois, lord of the castle of Morois, who possessed five hundred pounds worth of land, the best situated that ever were. He had a beautiful dwelling surrounded by high walls, with deep ditches, recently made, and at the foot of the castle he was pleased to go for exercise.

It happened one day in the month of April, that magnificent season, when he rose early in the morning, tastefully dressed in a shirt of light and supple linen with a belt – I have seen many less beautiful. He had no mediocre distinction, for he had dressed in a surcoat of precious scarlet, lined with ermine fur. He was well shod, with beautiful lace up shoes that were cut very smart. Once dressed and shod, losing no time, he called his squire to bring him his horse. He wanted to go into the forest to hear the nightingale.

The young man obeyed without question his master's orders; he saddled the horse, adjusted the harness in the portrait, and when he had disposed the reins – the horse was far from dead with hunger, it had been well looked after, its coat was beautiful – he took it to his master without further word. The knight mounted, his squire fixed his golden spurs, then slipped his sword into its golden scabbard. This done, the knight left his dwelling without companions and went off straight at the amble, towards the forest, along the river, across a meadow covered with white, red and blue flowers.

The knight went at a good pace, and resolved not to return before hearing the song of the nightingale that he had not heard for a year. On the approach to the forest Lorois looked before him and saw very peacefully coming out up to 80 damsels, courtly and beautiful, richly dressed, without cloaks or headdress, but they had put on their heads crowns of roses and eglantines because of their sweet fragrance.

Many of them wore belts cut loose and others were without belts because of the heat, and to be more at ease had let their hair fall free round their ears, the length of their face, in lively colours. It was a very pleasant group to see, with their tresses interlaced with ribbons.

All had white palfreys which carried them so gently that seated on one of them, without seeing them in movement, one would have thought they stayed still, except that they went faster than the greatest Spanish horses at the gallop. Know that as far as Germany there was no duke or châtelaine so rich as to buy the bit the poorest of them had on her palfrey.

Each one had near her, mounted on a destrier, her lover, elegant, pretty, seductive, gay, who sang with all his heart. They were sumptuously dressed, each wore a cloak of precious embroidered silk, lined with ermine and a long train, their spurs fixed to their feet. The destriers they rode went quietly at the amble, and know that a rich king would not have been able to buy such harness.

There was no envy between them, for each one had his lover and took pleasure, with light heart, each to each. Some of the lovers embraced, it was truly a life of pleasure. At this sight Lorois crossed himself, telling himself it was a true marvel and he would never again see the like. At this, he saw coming from the forest 80 ladies, each one of them also had a lover, in the same state that I have already told you. They followed the others, full of joy.

A little after, a great noise was heard in the forest, and dolorous plaints arose. He saw a hundred young girls come from the forest, but each came alone, without male company, on black nags thin and famished. They were the prey of great torment. But know this, they had well deserved it, as you will hear me tell if you listen.

In this deep distress they trotted so hard that no-one in the world, wise or foolish, could support so rough a ride, if only for a league, even for 5000 marks of silver. The reins on their bits were of stems of rushes, impractical, and their saddles broken, ripped in more than a hundred places. Their saddle cushions were stuffed with straw, so well that one could easily have followed their tracks for ten leagues through the straw that had fallen from them.

Each rode without stirrups, they had neither shoes nor socks and were bare footed. Their feet were in a pitiful state, full of cracks. Dressed in black frocks, their legs were naked to the knees and their arms villainously uncovered to the elbows. It snowed and thundered on their heads, it was such a frightening storm that one could not even bear to see the suffering and the grief they endured night and day. Before this sight Lorois nearly fainted. He had hardly looked on all before he saw 100 men in the same torment as the damsels – their innards jolted by the roughness of their ride. Soon after that he saw a lady coming mounted on a nag that trotted so awkwardly – have no doubt – that her teeth chattered at risk of breaking.

The knight looked at her and decided to ask what these strange things were that had passed before his eyes. He vigorously spurred his horse, went to the lady and saluted her. The lady looked at him, and managed to returned his salute, with which she had much difficulty because of the trot of her horse. Even stopped, her heart could not have been less shaken, so much did her horse make little jumps up and down. No matter what knight might have mounted it, gripped the saddle or held on to the mane, shaken about high and low, he would have ended up thrown to the ground. The lady did not fall but she gave many sighs.

"Lady," the knight said to her, "if you please, tell me who are the people who have passed by here."

"I will tell you," she replied, "as well as I can, but it is difficult to speak and I must be quick. Those who went before were full of joy, for each leads the man for whom she has the greatest love in the world; she can to her liking embrace him, enlace him, caress him. They are those who have in their life loyally served Love, who have loved with all their heart and well observed his commandments. Love has rewarded them in dispensing joy to them; they are happy, nothing displeases them. Winter or storm, does not matter, they know only fine days; they can rest at their pleasure and repose and sleep.

"Those who followed with plaints and sighs, who trotted so roughly and in such painful torment, who had pale and wan faces and rode without a man at their side, are they who have never done anything for love and have never deigned to love. He now makes them pay for their pride and arrogance.

"Alas! I have also paid very dearly myself, never to have loved and now I regret it. In neither winter or summer will we have rest nor the calming of our sufferings. We were born under an evil star, strangers as we are to love.

"If a lady hears speak of us and our misfortunes, and knows no love in her life, be sure of it, she will join us and repent of it too late. For as the proverb says: 'Who shuts her stable too late will lose her horse, to her despair.' It is the same for the heart if repentance has been too late."

At this the lady concluded. Lorois had listened very attentively and learned the lesson well. The troop of damsels drew away and Lorois returned straight away to the castle of Morois. He took to heart the strange adventure and all that the lady had told him explaining its reason.

Henceforth he advised young girls and ladies and damsels to beware of the Trot; it is much more preferable to go at the Amble!

The Bretons made a lai of it and called it the Lai of the Trot.

THE FAERY LAIS *of*
MARIE DE FRANCE

THE BRETON LAI is usually associated with Marie de France, who made a collection of a dozen of them, although only three of them fall into the category of faery lais. She appears to have been an educated lady of good family, familiar with courtly life, probably that of the English court of Henry II – for she writes in the Norman dialect of Old French. Her being named as "of France" suggests that she was brought up in the Île de France, the area around Paris rather than the extensive country we know as France today.

She had, by her own admission, literary ambitions, and was responsible for three major works. First her collection of Breton lais, then a version of about a hundred of Aesop's fables, and finally the *Espergatoire* – or Legend of the Purgatory of St. Patrick. The first composed some time before 1189 and the last some time after that. All that we can say for certain is that she was active around the last third of the 12th century – with 1160 as the earliest possible date and 1215 the last.

Although she was evidently quite a linguist, familiar with Old English and Latin, it is unlikely that her lais were translations from Breton or Welsh (the two terms were virtually synonymous in her day). Her originals were more likely to have been popular renditions in Old French which she refined into courtly octosyllabic couplets for the edification of an aristocratic audience. Although a lai was traditionally a performance art, a narrative with musical accompaniment, Marie's carefully crafted verses seem also aimed at private reading.

Whilst her lais were not devoid of any faery element or accounts of the marvellous, her main interest was in the psychology of her characters. It is this which makes her work an important milestone in the development of European literature. Although the fact that her women characters tend to be more forceful than the men might be seen as parallel to faery tradition, for faery women seem to call the shots in any relationship with a human hero. (Although the occasional male faery – as in the lai of *Tydorel* – shows that they too can be pretty forceful when they choose to be!)

This however is also part of the general social trend in aristocratic circles of the time, an attempt at increasing empowerment by women.

Leading examples of this were contemporaries of Marie such as Eleanor of Aquitaine and her circle, with their espousal of the cult of Courtly Love which endeavoured to idealise the courtly lady, much as the Arthurian romances tended to idealise the knight. Real life in medieval times was considerably more brutish.

The three of Marie's lais that feature faery are *Guigemar*, *Lanval* and *Yonec*. Indeed *Lanval* is another version of the anonymous lai *Graelent* and comparison of the two provides an interesting contrast between the lai as narrated in a popular context and the lai as rendered into courtly literature. Another lai of Marie's that is closely derived from an anonymous one is her *Bisclavret*, which is similar to the version we give of *Mélion* – both are werewolf stories but Marie has excluded any hint of a faery element, so we do not include it here. She was, in this respect, similar to her contemporary courtly writer, Chrétien de Troyes, who in his Arthurian romances tended to secularise much of the original faery element that he found in his originals.

However, when it comes to her depiction of faery characters we can do no better than allow Marie to speak for herself in the three of her lais that follow. They are perhaps the closest that the literary world has come to a valid account of faery. By the time of Shakespeare and Drayton we have them downgraded to cobwebby fantasy (although *A Midsummer Night's Dream* and *The Tempest* hint at some pretty feisty characters) and eventually to Victorian nursery whimsy before the Celtic resurgence at the turn of the 19th and 20th centuries with figures such as Yeats, George Russell and Fiona Macleod. Again, let it be said, with a resurgence of Celtic mythology! Although that has been labelled (with a certain hint of derision) as the Celtic Twilight, in fact, with the growing interest that is now manifest, it might better have been regarded as a new Celtic Dawn!

X

ALTHOUGH THE WORD faery is not mentioned in this lai of Marie de France, apart to say at one point that the heroine is as lovely as one, faery elements are jumping off the page, despite having been secularised by Marie in much the same way that Chrétien de Troyes secularised faery elements in his Arthurian romances, depicting faery guides as human damsels.[1]

Thus we have a talking stag (or rather a hind that has, contrary to all biological laws, the antlers of a stag) and is not only white, the faery colour, but capable of human speech and powers of prophecy concerning the hero's fate.

Then we have a magical ship that acts as a ferry between human and faery worlds, steering and setting sail by its own volition, including being in the right place at the right time. It is the traditional metaphysical ferry without the traditional ferryman, or at any rate without him being visible.

What is particularly remarkable about it is its similarity to the Ship of Solomon that appears in the later Graal romances – such as the one that took the three Graal winners Galahad, Percival and Bors to the Graal kingdom of Sarras. Yet Marie is writing some time before – which suggests that this is material that was already circulating well before the Graal romances, as we have them, were written.

This develops into another powerful traditional image when Guigemar himself becomes the wounded knight sleeping on the bed[2] within the magical ship to be discovered by the maidens. The fact that his wound is in the thigh marks another resonance with Graal imagery, with which Marie seems to have been familiar, even if not much concerned about its possible significance.

---

1   For details of this see *The Faery Gates of Avalon* by Gareth Knight (R. J. Stewart Books, 2008).
2   For significance of this, particularly in ballad tradition, see *The Underworld Initiation* by R. J. Stewart (Aquarian Press, 1985).

There is a considerable mix in Marie's sources, and it seems that she simply included anything she had come across that might be useful to garnish a story, without any thought of any possible deeper significance.

Her faery, ostensibly an ordinary human damsel, is quite capable of performing the supernormal feat of being able to tie a knot that no one but she can untie. Although her lover Guigemar proves capable of fashioning a chastity belt from which his lover cannot be released by anyone but himself.

Marie de France's magpie mind collects a whole series of images from various sources. The heroine's situation of being sequestrated by an old and jealous husband terrified of being cuckolded is a perennial situation in theatrical comedy, that goes right back to classical times and is still with us today.

Marie includes the somewhat bizarre decoration of the lady's room in which the figure of Venus, the goddess of love, predominates. Although at first sight this might seem to be in the nature of the mildly pornographic, its message is somewhat different, for it shows a book by the Roman writer Ovid being condemned and consigned to the flames. This would appear to have been his book *Amores*, which was highly popular at the time that Marie wrote, insofar that it influenced the cult of Courtly Love. Ovid's work was a comic, partly cynical, partly satirical guide to the arts of seduction – though with no latter day 12th century nonsense about putting the lady on a pedestal, even if the end in view was very much the same!

The eventual denouement, of undoing a knot in the tail of the hero's shirt and releasing the maiden from a chastity belt, may seem on the borders of the ludicrous, but nonetheless Marie plays to her strengths of depicting human psychology and character – which tends to be absent from the less sophisticated traditional anonymous lais.

IN THE TIME that Hoilas ruled the land, sometimes at peace, sometimes at war, the king had a baron who was lord of Líun. His name was Oridial and much prized by his lord, as he was a worthy valiant knight. He and his wife had two children, a son and a beautiful daughter. Noguent was the maiden's name, and Guigemar that of the son. No youth was more handsome in the whole kingdom and his mother and father greatly loved him. As soon as they could bear to part with him they sent him to serve another king. The young man was worthy and wise and much loved by all, and when he came of age the king dubbed him knight and endowed him richly with arms.

Guigemar left the court, dispensing lavish gifts before he left. He went off to Flanders to win renown, for there was always war and strife in Lorraine and Burgundy, Anjou and Gascony. At that time no knight could be found who was his equal. But Nature had given him a great fault – for he took no interest in love! If he had wanted, no lady or maiden on earth, however noble or beautiful, would have been unwilling to give him their love. Some even made advances to him but he showed no interest. So he was regarded a lost cause by friend and stranger alike.

At the height of his fame he returned to his homeland to see his lord and father and mother and sister, who had longed for his return. He had spent about a month with them when he took a fancy to go hunting. The night before, he summoned his knights and huntsmen and beaters, and in the morning went off into the forest, which gave him great pleasure. They started in pursuit of a great stag, the hounds were unleashed and the huntsmen ran ahead, but the young man lingered behind. A servant carried his bow along with his hunting knife and quiver – if the chance arose he wanted to shoot an arrow. Then he saw in the midst of a thicket a hind with a faun.

It was completely white and had stag's antlers on its head! As his dog barked it started forth, and he took aim and shot it. He struck it in the forehead but the arrow rebounded and pierced him through the thigh, into the very flesh of his horse. Forced to dismount, he fell back in the thick grass beside the beast he had shot. The wounded hind moaned in great pain and then spoke these words:

"Alas, I am dying. And you vassal, who wounded me, let this be your fate: you will never find a cure for it, by any herb or root or leech or potion, until you are cared for by one who will suffer more pain and anguish for your love than any woman who has ever been. And you will suffer likewise for her. So much that all who love, or who have loved, or who will ever love will marvel at it. Now go! And let me die in peace!"

Guigemar was dismayed by what he had heard and wondered wherever he could find such a cure, for he did not intend to lie there and die. He knew he had never found any woman he could love who might cure him of his suffering. He called out to his squire: "Friend, go quickly, and find my companions, I need to speak to them."

The squire rode off and he remained, lamenting his condition. Then with a strip from his shirt he tightly bound up his wound, mounted his horse, and left. He was keen to be on his way and not have any of his followers hinder or retain him.

A green path through the woods led him to an open space, and in the plain beyond he saw a mountain from which a stream was flowing down to an arm of the sea. Below the cliff was a harbour in which Guigemar could see the sail of a single ship. It was well prepared, so tightly caulked inside and out it was impossible to see any join. There was no peg or rail on deck that was not made of ebony, and the sail was of silk, more beautiful when unfurled.

The knight was puzzled, he had never heard it said in town or country that a ship could dock here. He rode forward, dismounted, and still in great pain, went aboard, expecting to find men in charge, but there were none. In the centre of the ship he found a bed whose posts and sidepieces were made in the style of Solomon, inlaid with gold, of cypress wood and ivory. A quilt of silk woven with gold lay upon it, the other bedclothes were beyond price. The coverlet of sable fur was lined with Alexandrian silk. And two candelabra of fine gold – the lesser worth more than a fortune – in which were lighted candles, were at the prow.

He marvelled at this and lay on the bed to rest, in great pain. But when he rose to leave the ship he found he could not do so, for it was on the high seas, speeding quickly before a favourable wind. There was no question of returning. Grief stricken, he did not know what to do. And no wonder he was dismayed, for his wound caused him great suffering and he had to accept his fate.

He prayed God to take care of him and bring him to safe haven and protect him from death. Then he lay back on the bed and slept. But the worst was over, for by evening he arrived at the place where he could be cured, before an ancient city, the capital of that kingdom.

The lord who ruled there was a very old man, whose wife was a lady of high birth, noble, courtly, beautiful and wise. He was extremely jealous by nature, as are all old men, dreading to be made a cuckold. Such is the perversity of age. He did not take the task of guarding her lightly. In a garden at the foot of the keep was an enclosure with a thick high wall of green marble. There was only one entrance, guarded night and day, and the other side was surrounded by the sea, impossible to get in or out except by boat should the need arise in the castle.

The lord had built within the enclosure a secure place for his wife – a chamber of incomparable beauty. At its entrance was a chapel, and the chamber itself skilfully painted all round, with Venus, the goddess of love, illustrating the nature and obligations of love – how it must be observed in loyalty and spirit of service. The book of Ovid which teaches the art of seduction was shown being cast into a blazing fire, excommunicating all who read the book or adopted its teachings.

In this room the lady was imprisoned. Her lord had provided a maiden to serve her, a noble intelligent girl who was his niece, his sister's daughter. The two loved each other dearly and when the husband was away she remained with her until his return. No man or woman could gain access to this place. An old priest with hoary white hair guarded the gate; he was also a eunuch, or he would not have been trusted. He recited the divine service and served at table.

That day, in the early afternoon, the lady had made her way into the garden, fallen asleep after her meal, and then gone in search of recreation together with her maiden. They looked towards the sea and saw the ship on the waves, but as it sailed into harbour could see no one steering it. The lady was afraid and turned to flee, her face flushed, but the maiden, who was bolder, comforted and reassured her. They hastened to the ship and the maiden, taking off her cloak, boarded the beautiful craft. She found no living thing apart from the sleeping knight, but seeing him so pale thought that he must be dead.

She stopped, looked and then turned, calling hastily to her lady telling her all she had seen, lamenting the dead body. Her lady replied,

"Let us go back together. If he is dead we will bury him – our priest will help us. But if he is alive he may speak to us."

They went back on board without delay, the lady first with the maiden following. Once on board the ship she stopped before the bed and looked down at the knight, grieving over his body and handsome face, filled with sorrow deploring the loss of his young life. She put her hand on his chest and felt it was warm! That his heart was beating beneath his ribs.

The sleeping knight awoke, saw her and greeted her cheerfully, knowing he must have come to shore. The lady, tearful and concerned, replied politely and asked how he came to be there, what country he had come from and if he was a victim of war.

"Lady," he said, "that is not so. But as you ask I will tell you the whole truth. I have come from Brittany where I was hunting in the woods today. There I shot a white hind but the arrow rebounded and pierced me through the thigh. I think a cure is impossible, for the hind lamented and spoke to me, cursing me and swearing that my only cure could be through a damsel. And who knows where she can be found?

"But when I heard my fate I hurried out of the wood, saw this ship in a harbour and foolishly went aboard. It sailed off quickly with me still on it and now I don't know where I am or what this city is called. Fair lady, I beg you in God's name try to help me, for I know not where to go or how to steer the ship."

She replied "My dear sir, I will tell you gladly. This city is my lord's and he rules the country round about. He is a rich man and noble but very old and fearfully jealous. To protect my honour he has imprisoned me in this enclosure. There is only one entrance and an old priest guards the gate – God grant that he burn in hell! I am shut in here day and night and dare not leave unless he calls for me. Here I have my bedroom and chapel, together with this damsel. If you wish to remain until you can move we will willingly shelter you and serve you wholeheartedly."

When he heard these words he thanked the lady politely and said he would stay with her. With some difficulty they helped him rise from the bed and took him to the lady's room and laid him on the maiden's bed behind a canopy that served as a curtain in the room. They brought water in golden bowls and washed his wounded thigh with a fine piece of white linen, removed the surrounding blood, and bound it tightly. They treated him with great care and when their evening meal was served the maiden kept sufficient for the knight's needs, so he was well provided with food and drink.

But love had now pierced him to the quick and his heart was pounding, for the lady had wounded him so deeply that he forgot about his homeland. He felt no pain from his wound yet sighed in anguish. He asked the maiden who served him to let him sleep. When he had dismissed her she returned to her mistress, who was now affected by the ardour which Guigemar had kindled in her heart.

The knight remained alone, mournful and downcast. He did not know the cause but at least he knew that if he were not cured by the lady he would surely die. "Alas," he said, "what shall I do? I will go to her and ask her to have mercy and pity on this forlorn wretch. If she refuses my prayer and is proud and hard then I shall die of grief and languish forever from this ill."

Then he sighed, for a new thought struck him, that suffering was inevitable and there was no alternative. All night he lay awake, sighing in anguish, as in his heart he recalled her words, her appearance, her sparkling eyes, her beautiful mouth, until the pain she caused reached right down to his heart. In a whisper he begged her mercy and almost called her his beloved.

If he had known her feelings and how love was afflicting her as well, he would, I think, have been happy. A little comfort would have come his way to ease the suffering which drained his face of colour. If he felt sad from loving her, she was certainly no better. Next morning she rose before dawn, bewailing having spent the night awake from this love that tortured her.

The maiden who was with her could see from the appearance of her lady that she loved the knight but did not know whether he loved her in return. So the maiden went to see the knight. As she sat upon his bed he said, "My friend, is my lady gone? Why did she rise so early?" Then he fell silent and sighed.

The maiden replied, "Sir, you are in love. Mind you do not hide it for too long! Your love may well have found a true home. Whoever loves a lady must keep her ever in his thoughts, then love will be right and proper if you are faithful. You are handsome and she is beautiful."

He replied to the maiden, "I am enflamed with love. I shall be in a sorry plight if I do not find relief. Tell me my sweet friend! What should I do about this love?" The maiden, courteous and noble, tenderly comforted the knight and assured him of her help in every way.

When the lady had heard mass she returned, and mindful of her obligations, wished to know how the knight was doing, whether he was awake or asleep. The love for him that had entered her heart had not abated. The maiden called on her to go to the knight – she would have ample time to reveal her feelings to him, no matter what the consequences.

He greeted her and she him, both in great distress, but he did not dare ask anything of her as he was a stranger in a foreign land. He was afraid that if he spoke of his feelings she would hate him and send him away. But he who does not let his infirmity be known can scarcely expect a cure! Love is an invisible wound within the body that has its source in Nature. It is a long lasting ill, the butt of jokes for many, such as those ignoble courtiers who philander round the world and then boast of their deeds. That is not love but folly, wickedness and debauchery. A loyal partner once discovered should be served, loved and obeyed.

Guigemar was very much in love and either had to find relief or be forced to live a life of misery. Love emboldened him to reveal his feelings to her. "Lady," he said, "I am dying because of you, my heart is giving me great pain. If you are not willing to cure me then it must end in my death. I am asking for your love, fair one, do not refuse me!"

When she heard these words she replied fittingly and lightly "Such a decision would be over hasty. I am not accustomed to such a request."

"Lady," he said, "in God's name have mercy. Do not be distressed if I say that a woman who is fickle and likes to extend courtship for her own esteem will not let a man know she has experienced the pleasures of love. But a well intentioned lady who is worthy and wise, if she finds him to her liking, should not be too harsh to a man. She should love him and enjoy his love before anyone knows of it, and they will greatly profit. Fair lady, let us end this talk."

The lady recognised the truth of his words and granted him her love without delay. He kissed her and henceforth was Guigemar at peace. They lay together, kissing and embracing. May the final act engaged by others give them great pleasure!

For a year and a half Guigemar was with her. Their life together gave them great delight. But Fortune, mindful of her duties, can soon turn her wheel to make one fall and another rise. And so it was the case with them, for they were soon discovered.

One summer morning the lady lay with the young man, kissed his mouth and face, then said, "My fair sweet friend, my heart tells me I am about to lose you. We are going to be discovered. If you die, I wish to die too, and if you escape you will find another love and I shall remain here grief stricken."

"Lady," he said, "Do not say such things! May I have no joy nor peace if ever I turn to another. Do not be afraid!"

"Beloved, give me assurance of that! Hand me your shirt. I shall tie a knot and give you leave, wherever you may be, to love the woman who can untie it."

He gave it to her, made his pledge, and she tied the knot in such a way that no woman could undo it without the help of scissors or knife. She gave him back the shirt and he took it on the understanding that she would make a similar pledge to him by means of a belt she would gird about her bare flesh and draw tightly round her loins, and allowed her to love any man who could open the buckle without tearing or breaking it. Then he kissed her and let the matter drop.

That day they were discovered, seen by a cunning chamberlain sent by her husband. He wished to speak to the lady, but as he could not enter her chamber peeked through the window and saw them, and reported it to his lord. When the lord heard this it gave him more pain than he had ever known. He summoned three trustworthy men and went to the chamber forthwith, had the door broken down and discovered the knight. Whereupon in great anger he ordered him to be killed.

Guigemar stood up, quite unafraid, and seized a large fir wood pole used for hanging clothes, and waited for them, intending to make someone suffer. Before any of them got near him he would have maimed them. The lord looked at him intently and asked who he was, where he was from and how he had entered.

Guigemar explained how he came, how the lady had kept him, all about the prophecy of the wounded hind, of the ship and his wound, and that he now was in the lord's power. The lord replied he did not believe him, but if things were as he said and he could find the ship, he would put him out to sea. He would be sorry if he survived and glad if he drowned.

When he had given this assurance they went to the harbour, found the ship and put him aboard. The ship set sail without delay, to take him back to his own country. The knight sighed and wept, lamenting the lady frequently and praying Almighty God to bring him a quick death without reaching land if he could not see his lover again, whom he desired more than life itself.

His grief was unabated until the ship arrived in port where it had first been found, close to his homeland. He disembarked as quickly as he could and recognised a young man following after a knight, leading his charger. He called out to him. The valet looked round, and when he saw his lord dismounted and offered him the horse, and they rode off together.

All his friends were full of joy that he had been found. He was highly regarded in his land but was constantly sad and downcast. They wanted him to take a wife but he would not think of the idea. He would never take a wife unless she could untie the shirt without tearing it. The news travelled through Brittany and there was no lady or maiden who did not make the attempt – but they were all unsuccessful.

Now I must tell you about the lady whom Guigemar loved so much. On the advice of his barons, her husband imprisoned her in a tower of dark marble. She suffered during the day and even worse at night. No man could describe the great pain, agony, anguish and grief that the lady suffered in the tower.

For two years or more she knew no joy nor pleasure and often mourned her lover: "Guigemar, lord, how sad I am that I ever met you. I would rather die a speedy death than suffer this any longer. Beloved, if I could escape I would go to where you put to sea and drown myself."

Then she went to the door, and found no key or bolt. Thus she had the chance to escape. No one hindered her as she went to the harbour and found the ship, anchored to the rock where she intended to drown herself. Seeing it, she went aboard, with only one thing in mind, that her beloved had been drowned.

Suddenly she found she could not stand upright. If she could have reached the side she would have thrown herself overboard but the ship had set sail, carrying her quickly away. It came to port in Brittany beneath a fine strong castle. The lord of the castle was called Meriadus. He was warring against his neighbour and had risen early in the morning to muster his forces to attack his enemy. Standing by a window he saw the ship arrive. He went down the steps, summoning his chamberlain. They hastened to the ship, climbed a ladder and boarded it, and there found the lady, who was as lovely as a faery.

Taking her by the cloak he took her off to his castle, delighted with his discovery. As she was extremely beautiful he knew that whatever the reason for her being on the ship, she must be of noble lineage. He conceived a love for her greater than for any other woman.

He had a younger sister who was very beautiful to whom he entrusted the lady, who was well served and honoured, richly dressed and attired, but always downcast and sad. He often went to speak to her for he loved her with all his heart, and begged for her love but she remained indifferent. Instead she showed him the belt and said she could only love the man who could undo it without tearing it.

When he heard this he replied angrily "There is also in this land a knight of very great renown who refuses in a similar way to take a wife, because of a knotted shirt which cannot be untied except by scissors or knife. I think it must have been you who tied that knot."

When she heard this she sighed and almost fainted. He seized her in his arms, cut the lacing of her tunic and tried to undo the belt, but to no avail. Then all the knights in the land were summoned to try. Thus things remained for a long time until Meriadus proclaimed a tournament against his enemy. He summoned his knights and retained them, confident that Guigemar would come, whom he asked as a friend and companion, promising him reward if he came to his aid.

He arrived richly attired with more than a hundred knights and Meriadus lodged him with great honour in his tower. Then he called for his sister to greet him, sending two knights with orders that she should adorn herself and come forward, bringing the lady he loved so much. She obeyed his command, and richly dressed and hand in hand they entered the hall, the lady still pale and sad.

On hearing Guigemar's name she lost her balance and if she had not been held would have fallen to the ground. The knight rose to greet them, saw the lady and stared at her appearance and manner, stepping back a pace. "Is this," he said, "my sweet friend, my hope, my heart, my life, my beautiful lady who loved me? Where has she come from? Who brought her? But these must be foolish thoughts, for I know it cannot be she. Women can look alike and my mind is disturbed for nothing. But since she resembles the one for whom my heart trembles and sighs I shall gladly speak with her."

The knight then went forward, kissed her and sat beside her. He spoke no word but to ask her to be seated. Meriadus looked on at them, very unhappy at how things appeared. Laughingly he called to Guigemar. "Sir," he said, "if you wish, let this maiden try to undo your shirt!"

He replied, "I accept," and summoned the chamberlain who looked after the shirt and ordered it to be brought.

It was given to the maiden but she did not untie it. She recognised the knot easily but her heart was too full of anguish. She would have been willing to try if she could and she dared. Meriadus realised this and it grieved him. All he could do was say "Lady, try to undo it!"

When she heard the command she took the shirt and untied it easily to the knight's astonishment. He recognised her, but all the same was not completely convinced. He addressed her with these words: "Beloved sweet creature, tell me true, let me see your body and the belt with which I girded you." He placed his hands on her hips and found the belt.

"Beloved," he said, "how fortunate I have found you like this. Who brought you here?"

She told him the grief, the great pain and sadness of the prison where she had been, and how things turned out. How she made her escape intending to drown herself but found the ship and gone on board and arrived at this port. How the knight had retained her and treated her with great honour but every day asked for her love. Now she was once more full of joy.

"Beloved, take your sweetheart away!"

Guigemar arose. "Lords," he said, "listen to me. I have found a friend whom I thought I had lost. I implore that Meriadus restore her to me in his mercy. I will become his vassal and serve him for two or three years with a hundred knights or more."

But Meriadus replied "Guigemar, fine friend, I am not so in need of help to fight my wars that you should ask this of me. I found her. I shall keep her, and defend her against you."

When he heard this Guigemar quickly ordered his men to mount, and left, issuing a challenge. It grieved him much to leave his beloved.

He took from the town every knight who had come to the tournament, and each one pledged his support. They would go wherever he went and any who failed to come would be in disgrace.

That night they arrived at the castle of Meriadus' enemy. The lord lodged them, happy to have Guigemar and his assistance. He realised the war was over.

Next day they rose early. Everyone in lodgings equipped himself and made a noisy exit from the town, Guigemar out in front. They reached the castle and attacked it but it was strong and they could not take it. Guigemar besieged the town and would not leave until it was taken. His friends and followers increased in number till all inside were starved. Then he captured and destroyed the castle and killed the lord within.

With great joy he took away his lover and now his troubles were over. This story I have told you of Guigemar was made into a lai which, when accompanied by harp and rote, is very pleasant to hear.

XI

Lanval

ARIE's *Lanval* is of particular interest from a literary point of view because it is a version of the anonymous lai of *Graelent*. It will be noticed that, no doubt with an eye to what is currently of popular interest, she sets the action in the court of King Arthur. Thus the rather dubious character of the queen is foisted upon Guenevere – although she is not mentioned by name.

Marie's treatment of the story is somewhat more sophisticated than the anonymous version and she shows a considerable knowledge of courtly protocol, particularly in the field of the administration of justice. It is debatable if this adds very much to the story but she uses it quite skilfully to prolong the dramatic tension towards the end.

Although she does not mention the word, Lanval's lover is obviously a faery, with her powers of providing great wealth and ability and to appear to her lover unseen or heard by others. Again we have the strict application of a faery prohibition or *geiss* which is uncompromisingly applied.

With a feminine eye for fashion perhaps, Marie's faeries tend to be dressed quite sexily, with varying exposure of bare flesh. An interesting feature, again evoking a dim Graal memory, is the first appearance of the faery's two servants with one bearing a golden bowl and the other a towel or napkin. Gold does tend to be somewhat indiscriminately applied to faery décor but the mention of golden bowls, not only here but elsewhere in the lais we have provided, has a resonance with the tradition found in the so-called *Elucidation* of Chrétien de Troyes' Graal romance of there originally having been maidens within wells who provided food for wanderers in the forest in golden bowls. Possibly an early tradition of faery lore.

Marie differs slightly at the end of her lai regarding the fate of the hero. Lanval is not required to go through the dramatic scenario of being half drowned in the river between the human and faery worlds before being taken off to Faeryland – and the folklore element of the grieving horse is also omitted. She may have realised that as it was a faery horse in the first place, there ought to have been no problem in its crossing the river to join its master. Or perhaps she just thought it an unnecessary coda to the human interest, or maybe never heard this version at all!

WILL TELL YOU THE STORY of another lai, just as it happened, about a noble young man called Lanval in Breton.

The worthy and courtly King Arthur was staying at Carlisle because the Picts and Scots were ravaging the country, entering the land of Logres and laying it waste. At Pentecost he gave many rich gifts to counts and barons and those of the Table Round – no greater company in all the world – and distributed wives and lands to all who had served him, save one.

This was Lanval, whom he did not remember, for no one had put in a good word for him, for many were envious of his valour, generosity, beauty and prowess. Some made out they liked him but would not have been sorry if things turned out badly for him. He was the son of a king of high lineage, but far from his inheritance, and he had spent all his money, for the king gave him nothing. Lanval did not ask but was sad and forlorn in his plight. Do not be surprised, my lords, a stranger without friends can be very downcast in another country if he does not know where to turn to find help.

The knight whose tale I tell had served the king well and one day mounted his horse to ride in the countryside alone. He left the town and came to a meadow where he dismounted by a stream, for his horse had begun to tremble violently. So he unbridled it and left it in the middle of the meadow to roll on its back. Then he folded his cloak as a pillow and placed it under his head, sad because of his troubles and seeing nothing to ease them.

Lying thus, he looked along the river bank and saw two damsels approaching, more beautiful than any he had ever seen. They were richly dressed in dark purple tunics tightly laced. The older one carried golden dishes, well and finely made, and the other carried a towel.

They came straight to where the knight lay, and Lanval, who had been well taught, stood up to meet them. The first one greeted him and told him this message: "Sir Lanval, my damsel, who is very worthy, wise and fair, has sent us for you. Come with us and we will take you to her safely. See, her tent is near."

The knight went off with them, disregarding his horse which was grazing in the meadow. They led him to a tent which so beautiful and well appointed that neither Queen Semiramis at the height of her power and wisdom nor the Emperor Octavian could have afforded even a part of it. It had a golden eagle on the top, and I do not know the value of ropes or poles that supported it, save no king on earth could have afforded them. Inside the tent was a maiden, and no lily flower or rose bud when it first appears in summer could have outmatched her beauty.

She lay on a fine bed – the coverlet was worth a castle – clad only in her shift. Her body was well formed and proportioned under a costly mantle of white ermine lined with Alexandrian purple to avoid the heat of the sun, but all the rest of her was uncovered, her face, neck and breast whiter than a hawthorn flower.

The knight came forward, called by the maiden, and sat before her bed.

"Lanval," she said, "fair friend, I have come in search of you from a far country. If you are worthy and courtly, no emperor nor count nor king could become as happy as you. For I love you above all else."

He looked at her and saw that she was beautiful. Love's dart so pricked him that his heart was set alight. He replied to her in a seemly way. "Fair lady," he said, "if it pleases you to grant me the joy of your wanting to love me, you could ask for nothing that I would not do my best to give you, whether it were foolish or wise. I shall do as you bid, and abandon all others for you. I will never want to leave you, for you alone I desire."

When the maiden heard these words that he loved her so, she gave her love and her body to him. Now Lanval was on the right path!

She also gave him the boon that he could wish for nothing that he could not have, however generously he gave or spent. She would provide him with enough, and see he was well lodged, and the more gold and silver he spent, the more he would have. "But my beloved," she said, "I admonish, order and beg you not to tell this to anyone. For you would lose me for ever if our love became known. You would never be able to see me or embrace me again."

He replied that he would do all that she commanded. He lay beside her on the bed and now was very well lodged. They remained together all the afternoon until evening and he would have stayed longer if he had been able and his lover allowed him.

"Beloved," she said, "arise! You can stay here no longer. Go from here and I shall remain, but whenever you wish to see me, wherever you may be, I shall not fail to come and do your bidding. And no one save you will see me or hear my voice."

When he heard this he was well pleased, kissed her and arose. Those who had led him to the tent dressed him in rich clothes, and when he was dressed anew there was no man on earth more handsome. They brought him water to wash his hands and a towel to dry them, then brought food, which was not to be disdained. He took his supper with his lover, they were courteously served and dined joyfully. One dish in abundance that greatly pleased the knight was his lover whom he often kissed and closely embraced.

When they had risen from the table they brought his horse, well saddled and richly caparisoned. He took his leave, and went back towards the city, often looking behind him, for he was greatly disturbed when he thought about his adventure, and uneasy at heart, for it seemed too good to be true.

But when he came to his lodgings he found all his men finely dressed, and that night he offered lavish hospitality and none knew how this came to be. There was no knight in town in need of shelter whom he did not invite and serve richly and well. He gave costly gifts. Freed prisoners. Clothed the jongleurs. Performed many honourable acts. There was no friend or stranger to whom he would not have given. And Lanval had great joy and pleasure by day and by night, for he could often see his beloved, whenever he desired.

In the same year, after the feast of St John, as many as thirty knights had gone to disport in a garden under the tower where the queen was staying. Gawain was with them and his cousin, the fair Yvain. The noble and worthy Gawain, who endeared himself to all, said "In God's name, sirs, we treat our companion Lanval very badly.

He is so generous and worthy and his father a rich king, yet we have not brought him with us." So they returned and went to his lodgings and persuaded him to go with them.

The queen, who was reclining at a window in the tower along with three ladies, caught sight of the party and saw and recognised Lanval. She called to one of her ladies to summon the most elegant and beautiful damsels to join her down in the garden where the others were. She took more than thirty with her and they went down the steps to where the knights came to meet them, happy at their coming. They took them by their hands and the conversation was not uncourtly. But Lanval withdrew to one side, far from the others, for he was impatient to meet his lover, to kiss and embrace her, and cared little for the joy of the others when he could not have his own pleasure.

When the queen saw him alone she straight away approached and spoke to him, opening her heart. "Lanval, I have honoured and cherished you much from afar. You may have all my love if you desire! I freely grant it to you and you should be very glad to have it."

"My Lady," he said, "let me be! I have no desire to love you. I have long served the king and could not betray his faith in me. Neither you nor your love will ever lead me to wrong my lord."

The queen became angry and distressed, and spoke unwisely. "Lanval," she said, "I do believe you do not like this kind of pleasure. I have often been told that you have no desire for women. I suppose you have well groomed young men instead and enjoy yourself with them. Base coward, wicked recreant, my lord is extremely unfortunate to have allowed you near him; I think he could well have risked his salvation!"

When Lanval heard this he was distressed but not slow to reply, and said something he had cause to regret.

"My Lady," he said, I am not skilled in that profession. I love and am loved by a lady whom I prize above all others. And I tell you this, you can be sure that any of her servants, even the very poorest girl, is worth more than you, my Lady, in body, face, beauty, goodness and wisdom!"

Thereupon the queen left him and went to her room crying, very distressed and angry that he had humiliated her in this way. She took to her sick bed, never, she said, to get up again until the king saw justice was done in regard to her complaint.

When the king returned from the woods after a very happy day and entered the queen's rooms, as soon as she saw him she complained aloud, fell at his feet, cried for mercy, and said that Lanval had shamed her. He had sought her love and because she refused him had insulted her deeply. He boasted to have a lover so well bred, noble and proud that her chambermaid, the poorest servant she had, was worthier than the queen.

The king grew angry and swore that if Lanval did not defend himself in court he would be burned or hanged. Then he left the room, summoned three of his barons and sent them for Lanval, who was already in great pain. For he had returned to his lodgings and realised he had lost his lover by revealing their love.

Alone in his room, anguished and distraught, he called to her repeatedly but all to no avail. He sighed and lamented, fainting from time to time, and called on her a hundred times to have mercy and speak to him. He cursed his heart and his mouth – and it was a wonder he did not kill himself. But his cries were not loud enough, nor his agitation and torment such, that she would have mercy on him or even permit him to see her. Alas, what could he do?

Those that the king had sent arrived and told him to go to the court without delay, that the king had summoned him through them, for the queen had accused him. Lanval went sadly with them and would have been content for them to kill him. He came before the king sad, subdued and silent, betraying his great sorrow. The king said to him angrily "Vassal, you have wronged me greatly. You were very ill advised to shame and vilify me and to slander the queen. You boasted foolishly. For your lover must be very noble indeed for her handmaiden to be more beautiful and more worthy than the queen."

Lanval denied having offended and shamed his lord point by point. He had not sought the queen's love, but of what he had said he acknowledged the truth. And regretted that and had now lost for ever the lover of which he had boasted. He said he would do anything the court decreed but the king remained angry and sent for all his lords to advise him what he should do.

Together they fixed the day for a trial, and for Lanval to provide pledges to await the day of judgment and return. The court would then be larger for now only the household retainers were present. The barons returned to the king and explained their reasoning and the king asked Lanval for pledges. But Lanval was alone and forlorn, having no friend or relation to pledge for him. But then Gawain approached and offered to stand bail and all his companions did too.

The king said to them, "I entrust him to you on surety of all you hold from me, lands and fiefs, each man for himself."

When this had been pledged there was no more to be done. Lanval went to his lodging, the knights escorting him. They urged him not to be so sorrowful and condemned his foolish love. They went to see him every day, for they wished to ensure he was eating and drinking properly, afraid that he might harm himself.

On the appointed day the barons were assembled, the king and queen were there, and the guarantors brought to court. They were all very sad on Lanval's account. I think there were more than a hundred who would have done all in their power to have him released without trial because they thought he had been falsely accused. The king demanded a verdict according to the charge and rebuttal.

The verdict was in the hands of the barons, who considered their judgment all day, concerned that this noble man from abroad should be in such a plight. Some wanted to condemn him because it was the will of their lord. But the Count of Cornwall spoke:

"There should be no doubt on our part that, like it or not, the right must prevail. The king has accused his vassal, whom I heard you call Lanval, of a felony, and charged him with the crime of boasting about a love which has angered my Lady. Only the king is accusing him, so there ought to be no case to answer – were it not that one should honour one's lord in all things. But as the king had put the matter in our hands, an oath will bind him. If his lover comes forward, provides proof that what he said to incur the queen's displeasure is true, then he should be pardoned, since he did not say it simply to spite her. But if he cannot furnish proof then he should quit the king's service and be banished."

They sent word to Lanval and told him to send for his lover to defend and protect him. He told them this was impossible, that he would receive no help from her. The messengers returned to the barons to say that no help would be forthcoming. The king now pressed them for a verdict, as the queen was waiting.

As they were about to decide they saw two maidens arriving, on two fine ambling palfreys. They were extremely comely, clad only in purple taffeta next to their bare skin. The knights were very pleased to see them. Gawain and three other knights went to Lanval to tell him and pointed out the two maidens. They were glad, and strongly urged Lanval to say if one was his lover. But he told them he did not know who they were, where they came from or where they might be going.

They continued to approach, still on horseback, and dismounted before the dais where King Arthur was sat. They were of great beauty and spoke in courtly tones.

"Sir King, make rooms available and hung with silken curtains so that our lady may stay, if she wishes to lodge with you."

This he granted willingly and summoned two knights, who led them to upper rooms. For the moment they said no more.

The king now asked his barons again for their judgment and said they had angered him with the long delay in their response.

"Lord," they said, "we were deliberating, but because of the ladies we saw, we have not yet reached a verdict. Let us continue with the trial." So they assembled with some anxiety and there was a good deal of commotion and contention.

While they were in this troubled state they saw coming along the road two more fully accoutred maidens, dressed in Phrygian silk and riding Spanish mules. The vassals were glad of this and said to each other that the worthy and brave Lanval was saved. Yvain went to him with his companions.

"Sir," he said, "rejoice. Two very comely and beautiful damsels are coming, surely one must be your beloved. For the love of God speak!"

Lanval replied that he did not recognise either, nor did he know or love them.

When they arrived they dismounted before the king and many praised them highly for being fair of body, face and complexion, and judged them both more worthy than the queen had ever been. The elder was courteous and wise and delivered her message fittingly. "Sir king, put rooms at our disposal for the purpose of lodging our lady. She is coming here to speak to you." He ordered them to be taken to the others who had earlier arrived, and they left their mules.

As soon as they had gone the king ordered his barons to deliver their verdict. They had taken up too much of the day, and the queen who was waiting was getting angry.

Just as they were about to deliver their verdict they saw coming into the town another damsel on horseback. There was none more beautiful in the world. She was riding a white palfrey which carried her well and gently – its neck and head well formed – there was no finer animal on earth. It was so well equipped that no count or king on earth could have afforded it save by selling or pledging all his lands. The lady was dressed in a white tunic and shift that, laced right and left, revealed her sides. Her body was comely, her hips low, her neck whiter than snow on the branch, her eyes bright and face white, mouth fair and nose well placed, eyebrows brown and brow fair, her hair curling and almost blonde. Golden thread does not shine more brightly than the sun's rays reflecting the light from her hair. Her mantle was of dark silk with the skirts enfolded round about her. She held a sparrow hawk on her wrist and was followed by a hunting dog. There was no man in town, humble or powerful, old or young, who did not watch her arrival – and not one doubted her beauty.

As she slowly approached, the judges who saw her thought her a great wonder. No one who looked upon her could fail to have been inspired with great joy. Those who loved the knight went to him and told him that the maiden who was coming would, please God, deliver him.

"Lord and friend, here comes a lady whose hair is neither tawny nor brown. She must be the most beautiful woman in the whole world."

Lanval heard this and raised his head. He knew her well, and sighed. The blood rushed to his face and he was quick to speak.

"In faith," he said, "it is my love! I hardly care if anyone kills me if she shows me no mercy. But my joy is in just seeing her."

The lady entered the palace, where no one more beautiful had ever been seen. She dismounted before the king and in the sight of all let her cloak fall so that they could see her better. The king, who was well mannered, rose to meet her and all the others honoured her, and offered themselves or their servants when they had looked upon her and been struck by her great beauty.

She spoke thus, for she had no wish to remain:

"Sir King, I have loved one of your vassals, Lanval, whom you see there. He stands accused in your court and I do not wish him any harm because of what he said. You should know that the queen was wrong, as he never sought her love. As regards the boast he made, if he can be acquitted by me then let your barons release him!"

As the judges so recommended, the king granted that it should be. There was not one who did not consider that Lanval had been successfully defended. As all was resolved by their decision, the damsel now departed, and the king could not retain her or her servants.

Outside the hall was a great block of dark marble by which heavily armed men mounted their chargers. As they left the court Lanval climbed onto it and when the damsel passed leapt up on the palfrey behind her in a single bound. He went off with her to Avalon, which, so the Bretons say, is a very beautiful island.

Thither Lanval was borne and no one has since heard anything of him, nor can I tell you any more.

XII

ONCE AGAIN, as in Guingemar, we have the situation of a young lady married to a jealous old husband who keeps her imprisoned in isolation, although this time located in South Wales rather than Brittany.

The eponymous Yonec does not appear until almost the end of the lai, as interest centres upon his faery father, his sequestrated human mother, and the circumstances of how he was conceived. One might have expected the lai to be called after Yonec's father, Muldumarec, which is a very rare case in faery tradition of a faery being named.

We have in this lai another case in which we have a faery knight who comes to his human lover when she calls for him. It is also notable that the first occasion is a direct result of her prayers, in which she is plainly referring to a tradition of faery lovers coming to maidens. Thus, as in the lai of the Hawthorn, we have the implication that God is on the the lovers' side: in the Hawthorn to transport the maiden to a faery location, and in this case to evoke a faery lover who, he says, has long loved her from afar but could not come to her until she made the invocation. One might also wonder whether a human/faery relationship requires the initiative to be set up on the female side – be they human or faery.

As if the transformation of Yonec's father between hawk and knight were not evidence enough of his faery status (although a more common transformation, as in *Tyolet* or *Mélion* is between faery knight and stag) he evidently, like the traditional Celtic *sidhe* or Tuatha de Danann, lives in a land that is reached by going into a hill.

Once again we have an incidental symbolic scenario of a wounded knight on a bed, with a hint of a triple manifestation of this when Yonec's mother goes through the faery palace. On announcing their final separation at his death, the faery king, as he turns out to be, is also capable of prophecy – which might almost be interpreted as a curse.

He also gives her a magic ring that has a profound psychological effect upon her husband's memory, to enable her to continue living with him and also for him to think that the child is his own. Thus the end of the story comes after Yonec has been born, come to maturity and been knighted, and is able to exact due vengeance on his parents' behalf.

Using the sword his father has bequeathed him, Yonec cuts off his step-father's head on his faery father's tomb, upon which, after telling all, his mother has just expired. The faery world can be a very unforgiving one, although it could be argued that his step-father had asked for all he got by his cruelty to Yonec's parents. A lesson perhaps to possessive husbands everywhere in Marie of France's contemporary world of Courtly Love!

ow I HAVE BEGUN to write lais I shall not cease to try to relate the adventures I know. It is now my intent and desire to tell you of Yonec, how he was born, and how his father, whose name was Muldumarec, first met the mother who gave birth to him.

In Britain there lived a rich old man who held the fief of Caerwent and was acknowledged lord of this city that lay on the river Duelas, that once ships could reach. He was very old, and because his inheritance would be large, he took a wife to have children who would be his heirs.

The maiden who was given him was from a noble family, wise, courtly, extremely beautiful, and much loved by the rich old man for her beauty. But because she was so fair and noble he took great care to watch over her and locked her in his tower in a large paved chamber. He had a sister, old and widowed, with no husband, and placed her with the lady to keep her from going astray. There were other women I believe in a separate room, but the lady could never have spoken to them without the old woman's permission.

Thus he held her for seven years – they never had any children – and she never left the tower either for family or friend. When the lord had gone to bed neither chamberlain nor doorkeeper would have dared enter the chamber to light a candle before him. The lady was in great distress and wept and sighed so much that she lost her beauty, as happens to any who take no care of themselves. She would have preferred death to take her quickly.

It was the beginning of April when the birds sing their songs. The lord rose early in the morning and prepared to go into the woods. He made the old woman get up and lock the doors after him, and when she had done his bidding and he had left with his man, she took her psalter into the chapel from which she intended to recite.

The lady was left lying awake and weeping, waiting for the sunlight. She noticed the old woman had left the room and grieved, sighed and lamented tearfully.

"Alas," she said, "that ever I was born, my fate is hard indeed! I am a prisoner in this tower and death alone will free me. What is that jealous old man afraid of to keep me so imprisoned? He is extremely stupid and foolish, always fearing he would be betrayed. I cannot even go to church to hear God's service or talk to people and join them in amusement. Cursed be my parents and all who gave me to this jealous man. I pull and tug on a strong rope! He will never die. When he was baptized he must have been plunged in a river of hell!

"I have heard there used to be adventurers in this country to relieve the afflicted. Knights who discovered maidens to their liking, noble and fair, and ladies who found handsome and courtly lovers. There was no fear of reproach and none but they could see them. If that can be, and if it ever was, surely it could happen again? May Almighty God grant my wish!"

Having lamented thus she noticed the shadow of a large bird through a window but did not know what it could be. It flew into the room, had straps on its feet and seemed to be a hawk of five or six moultings. It landed before the lady and after it had been there for a while and she had closely regarded it, turned into a fair and noble knight.

The lady was astonished, her face flushed, she trembled and covered her head. The knight was extremely courtly and spoke to her first. "Lady," he said, "don't be afraid! The hawk is a noble bird, even if its secrets remain a mystery. Be assured you are safe and make me your beloved!

"This is why," he said, "I have come. I have loved you for a long time and desired you greatly in my heart. I have never loved any woman but you, nor shall I ever love another. Yet I could not come to you nor leave my country until you wished for me. But now I can be your lover!"

The lady was reassured, uncovered her head and spoke. She answered the knight and said she would make him her lover provided he believed in God, which would make their love possible. He was very handsome, never in her life had she seen such a handsome knight nor ever would again.

"Lady," he said, "you are right. I would not on any account want guilt, distrust or suspicion to attach to me. I do believe in the Creator who set us free from the sorrow in which our ancestor Adam put us by biting the bitter apple. He is, will be and has been life and light to sinners. If you do not believe me send for your chaplain. Tell him an illness has come upon you and you want to hear the service that God has established for the redemption of sinners. I shall take on your appearance, receive the body of Christ and recite all the creed for you. Never doubt me on that count!"

She replied he had spoken well. He lay down on her bed but did not attempt to touch, embrace or to kiss her.

When the old lady returned she found the lady awake and told her it was time to get up, she would bring her clothes. The lady said she was ill and asked for the chaplain to come quickly, for she feared she was dying.

The old woman said, "Be patient! My lord has gone to the woods and no one may enter here but me."

The lady appeared to become very afraid and pretended to faint. When she saw this the old woman was much alarmed, opened the door of the chamber and sent for the priest, who came as quickly as possible, bringing the corpus domini. The knight received it, drank the wine from the chalice, and the old woman shut the doors.

The lady now lay next to her lover. I never saw so fair a couple. When they had laughed and sported and exchanged confidences the knight took his leave, for he wanted to return to his country. She begged him gently to come back and see her often.

"Lady," he said, "whenever it pleases you, I shall be with you within the hour. But be careful we are not discovered. The old woman will betray us and keep watch over us night and day if she notices your love and will tell her lord about it. If this should happen as I say and we are thus betrayed I shall have no way of preventing my death." Thereupon the knight departed and left his love in great joy.

Next day the lady arose, quite recovered, and was very happy that week. She looked after herself and her beauty was greatly restored. Now she was more content to remain than to amuse herself in any other way, for she wanted to see her lover often and take her pleasure with him as soon as her lord had left. Night or day, early or late, he was hers whenever she wanted. May she, with God's grace, long enjoy her love!

The great joy she experienced on often seeing her lover caused her appearance to change. Her lord, who was very cunning, noticed she was different from her usual self. He was suspicious of his sister but spoke to her one day and said he was troubled that the lady dressed thus and asked what this might mean. The old woman did not know, for no one could speak to her nor did she have friend or lover. But she had noticed that she remained alone more willingly than before.

"In faith," he said, "I can believe that! Now you must do something. In the morning, when she has risen and you have locked the doors, pretend to go outside and leave her to be alone. But stay in a secret place and watch to see what it can be that makes her so joyful."

With this plan they parted. Alas, how ill served were they on whom they planned to spy and to betray. Three days later, I heard tell, the lord pretended to leave, telling his wife that the king had summoned him but he would soon be back. He then left the chamber and the old woman arose and hid behind a curtain where she could easily hear and satisfy her curiosity.

The lady lay without sleeping, for she greatly desired her lover, who came in no time at all. They were full of joy together, to talk and exchange glances until it was time to get up, for then the knight had to go. The old woman saw and noted how he came and went but was very much afraid because she saw him as a man and then as a hawk.

When the lord returned, who had not been far away, he was most distressed and quickly made traps to kill the knight. He had great iron spikes forged, the points sharper than any razor. When he had prepared and cut barbs in them he set them on the window close together, well positioned, where the knight passed when he came to see the lady. Oh God! If only he had known the treachery the villain was preparing!

Next morning the lord arose before dawn and said he was going hunting. The old woman went to see him off and then returned to bed, for dawn was not yet visible. The lady was awake, waiting for him she faithfully loved. She said he could come now and be with her at leisure. When she summoned him he left without delay and flew through the window. But the spikes were in front of it, one of them pierced his body, and the red blood flowed out.

When he realised he was mortally wounded he freed himself from the prongs, entered and sat on the bed beside the lady, covering the sheets with blood. When she saw the wound and the blood she was grievously alarmed. He said to her, "My sweet love, for love of you I am losing my life. I told you what would become of it, that your appearance would betray us."

When she heard this she fainted, and for a while seemed dead. He comforted her tenderly, saying that grief was of no avail, and telling her she was with child by him, and would have a worthy valiant son to comfort her. She was to call him Yonec and he would avenge them both.

He could remain no longer for his wound bled. He left her in great pain, and she followed him with loud cries. She escaped through a window and jumped and it was a wonder she did not kill herself for it was well over twenty feet from the ground.

Naked but for her shift, she followed the trail of blood which flowed from the knight on the path he was taking, to which she kept until she came to a hill. In this hill was an opening all covered with his blood but she could see nothing beyond it and assumed her lover must have entered there. She hurried in, but finding no light, followed a straight path until she emerged on the other side of the hill in a beautiful meadow.

There was a city nearby, completely enclosed by a wall, and not a house, hall or tower which did not seem to be of solid silver, and the state of their rooms were especially rich. Over toward the town were the marshes, the forest and the enclosures, and the other direction led towards the keep. A stream flowed all round where ships used to arrive, and where there were more than three hundred sails.

The gate downstream was unlocked and so the lady entered, still following the fresh blood through the centre of the town, up to the castle. No one spoke to her, for she met neither man nor woman.

She came to the paved entrance of the palace and found it covered in blood. She passed into a beautiful chamber and found a knight sleeping there, but did not know him and so went on to another larger chamber. Finding nothing there but a bed with a knight sleeping on it, she continued through and entered a third chamber and found her lover's bed. The parts of the bed were of pure gold, and I cannot guess the worth of the bedclothes. Candles lit by night and day were in candelabra worth all the gold in the entire city.

As soon as she saw the knight she knew him and approached in alarm, falling over him in a swoon. He who loved her deeply took her in his arms, lamenting their misfortune. When she had recovered he comforted her gently:

"Fair friend, in God's name take care. Go away! Fly from here! I shall die before dawn, and there will be such grief that if you are found here you will be put to torment. For my people will say they have lost me because of my love for you. I am sad and troubled for your sake."

The lady said to him "Beloved, I would rather die here, together with you, than suffer with my husband. If I go back to him he will kill me."

The knight reassured her, gave her a ring and told her that as long as she kept it her husband would remember nothing that had happened and would not keep her in custody. He gave and commended to her his sword and enjoined her to prevent any man from ever taking it, and to keep it for the use of her son when he had grown up and become a worthy and gallant knight. She would take him and her husband to a feast, and they would come to an abbey. At a tomb they would visit they would hear about his death and how he was unjustly killed. There she would give him the sword and tell him the story of his birth and who his father was. Then they would see what he would do.

When he had explained all to her he gave her a costly tunic and told her to put it on. Then he made her leave him. She went, wearing the ring and carrying the sword that comforted her. She left the city and had not gone half a league before she heard the mourning bells ringing and lamentations within the castle. She swooned four times with grief, but when she recovered went on towards the hill, passed through, and arrived back in her own country.

Afterwards she remained a long time with her husband, who made no accusations against her and neither mocked or slandered her.

Their son was born and well brought up, protected and loved, and they called him Yonec. In the whole kingdom there was found no youth so fair, worthy, valiant and generous. When he came of age they had him dubbed a knight. Now listen to what happened in the same year!

At the feast of St Aaron, that was celebrated in Caerleon and several other cities, the lord had been summoned with his friends. And as the custom of the country was, he took his wife and son and dressed himself richly. So it was they set out not knowing exactly where they were going. With them was a young lad who led them along a straight road until they came to a castle fairer than any other they had seen. Inside was an abbey with very holy people.

The squire who was taking them found them lodgings. In the abbot's chamber they were well served and next morning went to hear mass. Then they intended to depart, but the abbot came to talk to them and begged them to stay. He wanted to show them his dormitory, his chapter house, his refectory, and since they were well lodged the lord consented to stay.

That day after dinner they visited various rooms. First came the chapter house, where they found a great tomb covered with a band of striped brocade with rich gold material running through it. At the head, foot and sides were twenty lighted candles. The candelabra were of fine gold, and the censers, which were used during the day to honour the tomb, were of amethyst.

They asked those who came from the country of the tomb what man lay there. They began to weep and said through their tears it was the best knight, strongest and fiercest, fairest and most loved, who had ever been born. He had been king of that land, no one had been more courtly. But he had been destroyed at Caerwent for the love of a lady.

"We have never since had a lord. We have long awaited for a son he gave the lady, just as he said and commanded."

When the lady heard this news she called aloud to her son.

"Fair son," she said, "you have heard how God brought us here. It is your father who lies here, whom this old man unjustly killed. Now I commend and give you his sword, for I have kept it long enough."

For all to hear, she revealed to him how the dead knight had come to her and how her husband betrayed him. She told him the truth, then fell in a faint on the tomb and in the swoon died; she never spoke again.

When her son saw she was dead, he struck off his step-father's head with his father's sword and avenged his mother's grief. When what had happened was known in the city they took the lady in great honour and laid her in the tomb. They made Yonec their lord before leaving the place.

Those who heard this story long afterwards, composed a lai about the sorrow and grief the two had suffered for their love.

Summary Notes

THE WAY TO GET THE MOST from faery lais is simply to immerse yourself in the story and let the imagination run free. However, a little intellectual analysis may not go amiss and may serve as a guide, as long as we do not let it form into rules of the game – which in any case seem to be laid down on the faery side rather than the human. In the dozen lais we may note a few common characteristics, and others not so common. Such as: Location – Gender – Offspring – Circumstance – Common objects – Geiss – Destination – Birds and Beasts.

Location
Of the twelve lais that we have cited, most take place in Brittany (*Graelent, Guingamor, Tydorel, the Hawthorn, the Trot, Guigemar,* and *Doon* in part). The other part of *Doon* is in Scotland along with all of *Désiré* and *Lanval.* There are two in England (*Tydorel* and part of *Mélion*) and one in Wales (*Yonec*). The other part of *Mélion* is located in Ireland although it is possible that this location is really Faeryland.

In whatever land we happen to be, the presence of water seems particularly important. Faeries are found by springs or fountains in *Graelent* and *Guingamor*, and at a riverside in *Lanval.* A journey by sea in a magic ship occurs in *Guigemar,* and *Doon* and his bride are separated by the English Channel. A river appears as a definite frontier between human and faery worlds in *Graelent* and notably in the faery ford in *the Hawthorn.* Nor should we forget the importance of the lake in *Tydorel.* Indeed in Arthurian tradition the Lake is often a synonym for Faeryland – where the ladies of the lake come from, and to which Lancelot was abducted as a child, hence his being called Lancelot du Lac.

In almost every lai we have the forest as the location for faery activity, with the exception in our lais of *Doon, Yonec* and *Guigemar.*

Gender
The faeries are female in *Graelent, Guingamor, Désiré, Lanval* and the King of Ireland's daughter in *Mélion* and the damsel with the bratchet

in *Tyolet*, if they are indeed faeries, as seems probable. Also the lady who explains the meaning of the scenario in *the Trot*.

But we have male faery knights in *Tydorel, Tyolet, the Hawthorn*, and *Yonec*. It is debatable which of the two principal characters is the faery in *Doon* and in *Guigemar*. While there is a collection of both male and female faeries in *the Trot*, assuming that they are not just allegorical figures.

In the case of female faeries, those in *Graelent* and *Guingamor* appear naked in a pool by a spring, that in *Lanval* in a sumptuous tent by a river. *Désiré* meets his future faery wife in a leafy bower, whilst *Mélion* meets his wife while hunting in the forest. Indeed all these feminine encounters take place in a forest locale. An exception is the eventual wife of *Tyolet*, who turns up at King Arthur's court with the prospect of a quest for any knight prepared to take it up.

Faery knights tend to turn up in search of their paramours. The one in *Tydorel* seeks out his in a garden or orchard (the terms tend to be synonymous in lai tradition – with the orchard having the greater faery resonance deriving from Avalon being called the Isle of Apples) but seems most at home in a lake, to where his son eventually returns. In *Tyolet* a faery knight in the forest instructs the young hero about knighthood after transforming from the appearance of a stag. In *the Hawthorn* three faery knights arrive at the faery ford to confront the young hero and provide him with a test in arms. Whilst another transforming faery knight appears in *Yonec* in the form of a hawk at his chosen lady's window. Another assignation in a sequestrated lady's chamber occurs in *Guigemar* – although in this tale by Marie de France it is not clear if or which of the two protagonists is the faery – anyhow he is brought and eventually departs in a magic ship that later serves his lover.

Offspring
Children are born of some of the human/faery liaisons. A son and daughter to *Désiré*, two sons to *Mélion*, a son to *Doon*, the eponymous hero and his sister in *Tydorel*, whilst *Yonec* is also the son of a faery father and human mother.

Circumstance

How did meeting come about? The female faeries seem to have the power to attract their intended human lover to a place of seduction with the preliminary circumstance tending to be the human knight in some kind of trouble.

After which they not only give their sexual favours but provide abundant wealth to their chosen human partner. In the case of *Graelent* and *Lanval* their presence cannot to be seen or heard by any other human observer and they can come to him wherever he may be. *Désiré* only meets his faery lover by assignation in the forest (a synonym for fairyland). *Mélion* is openly married to his wife before she deserts him and goes back to Ireland/Faeryland.

Common objects

Golden bowls turn up carried by faeries on occasion which is an interesting feature in that in the so-called *Elucidation* to Chrétien de Troyes' *Conte del Graal* the origin of all the troubles prior to the Arthurian period came about when what seem to be proto-faeries appeared from wells in the forest bearing golden bowls for the sustenance of travellers. This came to an end when wicked King Amangons and his dastardly followers began to rape the maidens and carry off their golden bowls. The solution to this problem is held to be preserved in the Holy Graal traditions and the finding and restoration in Logres of the court of the Rich Fisher King.

Magic rings are often favoured by faeries and in the lais we have examples in *Désiré*, *Mélion* and *Doon*. Whilst the last mentioned is not particularly magical, the other two are particularly important, one as a token of the ongoing relationship, and the other – with its stones of red and white – the agency for shape shifting between man and wolf.

Geiss

The general prohibition placed upon a faery/human relationship is that it should be kept secret. This is the case in *Graelent*, *Désiré*, *Tydorel*, *Guigemar* and *Lanval*. *Mélion* seems a rare case of betrayal by a faery.

Destination

Most of the human heroes end up in fairyland. As in *Graelent*, *Guingamor*, *Désiré*, *Lanval* and *Yonec*. *Tyolet* possibly if his paramour is a faery. *Mélion* after his shabby treatment from the daughter of the King of Ireland returns home. Of the heroines, the queen in *Yonec* dies in Faeryland.

Birds & Beasts

Deer, boars, hawks and horses are commonly found connected with faery; all of which are connected in one way or another with hunting. Deer were popularly referred to in medieval times as "faery cattle" and generally appear as stags, although a hind is occasionally found, as in *Guigemar* even though it has a stag's antlers. Stags also appear in *Désiré*, *Tyolet* and *Mélion*, in the first two cases with a stag transforming into a faery knight. A fawn makes a brief appearance in *Guigemar* and a roebuck provides a meal for *Tyolet*.

Another commonly hunted beast that may have strong faery connections is the boar, which plays a major part in *Guingamor*, along with a hunting dog or bratchet, that is central to the action in *Tyolet*. The wolf in the form of a werewolf is central to the action in *Mélion*.

Hawks are also commonly found associated with faeries although apart from the remarkable case of *Yonec* where a faery transforms into one, the only other appearance in our lais is in *Lanval* where the faery appears at the end with a hawk upon her wrist, and it may be recalled that her tent had the figure of an eagle as its crest.

Horses were the principal form of transport in medieval times but remarkable ones appear in *Graelent*, which pines for its master lost to Faeryland, and in *Tydorel* where the faery's horse is capable of going under water, and for the remarkably speedy horse of *Doon*. In *the Hawthorn* the hero is presented with a faery horse that needs no feeding but must always be kept on the bridle. Whilst we should not forget the remarkable strangely trotting horses in *the Trot*.

The mule also appears as a favoured means of transport for some faeries, as in *Lanval*.

A horse, or boar or stag associated with faery is very often white, and sometimes horses or hounds have red ears, red and white being the traditional faery colours.

www.ingramcontent.com/pod-product-compliance
Lightning Source LLC
Chambersburg PA
CBHW030344030726
47499CB00003B/899